Mesquite

Creek

Ranch

Part 1

Mesquite Creek Ranch

Part 1

A Novel

By Charlene Reams Manning

ISBN-13: 978-0-578-62145-6

Mesquite Creek Ranch Part 1 Copyright 2019

Charlene Reams Manning

Picture on Cover by G Allen Penton

Picture of Author by Clint Reams

Dedication

I thank God for the family nest I lived in for the first nineteen years of my life. I began with my McLaughlin grandparents, who loom large in my life even now after they passed away. I learned much from them, sitting by a knee, riding in a pickup, helping with chores. My parents were examples: I learned from them what to do, what not to do. Sometimes it was taught with words and other times I learned from seeing their example.

Many of the things I wrote about in the two books were gleaned from memories of the McLaughlin foursome who grew together and stuck together for as many years as we had together. We learned from each other and grew into who we are.

In honor of my Chickasaw Daddy and Granddaddy, I applied to the Bureau of Indian Affairs for citizenship. Now, myself, my sons, and my grandchildren are registered citizens of the Chickasaw Nation.

Dedicated to all my McLaughlin kin,
especially my birth family:

Clinton Duke McLaughlin

Mary Cotton McLaughlin

and

Clinta "Mackie" McLaughlin

Thanks for the memories.

Acknowledgments

I want to thank the people who were a part of making this story come to life in writing.

My friend Bonnie Manning helped open my heart to the idea of writing a novel and provided valuable input for improving technique in my first attempt at faith-based fiction. She was also my editor, putting the polish on my work. I owe her and her husband Jeff a debt of gratitude for getting my books into print.

My son Clint Reams was a great encouragement to me as I hammered out the story of Mesquite Creek Ranch. He reminded me often, "Mom, you can do this!" and, "Time for a break, Mom." He also provided the back-cover photo.

I had feedback from longtime friends who reviewed the earliest chapters. They were helpful with those rough drafts, encouraging me to go on and make this story happen.

The One to whom I owe the greatest debt of all is the Lord. My gift of writing is from Him. I saw in my mind's eye and knew when the inspiration was coming from Him. It was more than what my own imagination could have accomplished.

Thank you, Father God!

Introduction

Writing is my calling, my pass time, and my joy! But the process of writing can be frustrating and is definitely hard work. Many hours were logged for me and those who helped me bring this project to the final product. It is my prayer that you, the reader will be blessed, taught, and even entertained by this story that God gave me to write!

When I felt the go-ahead from the Lord to jump into this project writing fiction, He reminded me of some notes I jotted down about twenty-five years ago. It was about a small town in Texas in the 1950's. A lengthy search produced the notes, but they were hardly anything more than the germ of an idea. I had a picture in mind of a creek with a child as the central character. And I still felt a "witness" in my spirit, concerning the potential with this lowly idea of a start.

As the writing began, there was a ranch with a creek, its own town, and a name. The characters took form, the story line began to appear. Writing fiction is more difficult than offering up books with information, facts, Scriptures, teaching and/or opinions.

This book (and its sequel) has every age reader in mind. It's a tale of life with its struggles and victories. It's a story, but still true to life's realities, the good and the bad. I hope it entertains my readers and leaves them with a feeling that life can present wonderful possibilities for happiness and peace. I pray a blessing on all those who read these books. Part Two will appear in the not-too-distant future.

~charlene reams manning

Chapter 1

I am Wes Redmond, author of this story of my adventures as I grew up on Mesquite Creek Ranch. I am a grown man now. Married. And I have children. I don't know why I'm making this memoir. It seems important that I do.

It was a glorious Texas Spring morning in April. The air still felt a little crisp. The bright green grass, glorious blankets of Bluebonnets and the budding green trees all spoke clearly to LIFE. It was and still is, my favorite time of the year.

With high hopes and not much sleep in the last 18 hours—Wesley Hunter Redmond, my Daddy Duke and my Mama Betty, went rolling through the gates of Mesquite Creek Ranch. I was eight and a half years old, and about as excited with this trip as anything I had ever done in my life.

The day before, we cleaned the place we had called home for a short while, packed up our '47 Ford pickup with our meager belongings, and took off into the great unknown!

Daddy had a plan. "We will drive straight through and only stop a few times for food and gas, and to let Mama drive so I can get an hour or two of sleep. We can't get a motel. Everything we own is in the back of this truck where thieves could get at it. We can't risk that."

I asked questions about the ranch and how this all came about. The name Mesquite Creek Ranch was my first question and right up Daddy's alley.

"What does Mesquite mean, Daddy?"

He smiled. "Well, its trees that grow in hot, dry places like Texas. Some people don't like them--they have mean thorns. But they're tough and can survive the worst heat and drought because their roots go very deep. At first, they're scrubby little brush plants. They grow up from beans the big trees drop. But in time they can become large, beautiful shade trees. The wind blows gently, the trees make a sweet, comforting sound."

"Mesquite wood makes a cozy fire inside, great campfire outside, and in the grill where we barbecue brisket. The smoke adds a delicious one-of-a-kind flavor to the meat."

My Daddy is a quiet man. He almost seems to work at saying the fewest words possible. Hearing him talk about trees, sounding forever more like an encyclopedia was a surprise.

We had the windows rolled down. The breeze made me think of summer coming. I was eager to hear the Mesquites making their sound with the wind. Summer would be hot and probably dry again. Texas was in a drought.

"Your Mama had a craving for brisket when she was expecting you! Isn't that right, Betsy?" Mama's name is Betty, but Daddy gave her that nickname.

Mama pushed her sunglasses up on top of her head, and chuckled. "I surely did. And, Wes that there is your dear ol' dad reminding me how fat I got before you were born! He's a real charmer, ain't he? And right now, Mr. Amateur Comedian, I'm hungry enough I could eat a whole jar of bread and butter pickles!"

Daddy threw his head back and hee-hawed. His brown eyes twinkled. I understood about Mama getting fat but could not imagine her that way.

I didn't get the joke about the pickles at all--or Daddy laughing like he did. They seemed to have a code all their own sometimes. Mama said I had big ears and was nosey. What did that mean? Daddy was still laughing a little. "Well, Darlin' you go on and break out the sandwiches and get us some Co-Colas!"

Mama opened up our little cooler and got out the sandwiches she made for the trip. She also had some Cokes in the ice which was a rare treat for us. We drank water or sweet tea at home.

It was a good lunch. After we ate, I got sleepy.

I woke when Daddy pulled into a gas station. Time for a bathroom break and getting the truck gassed up. Mama and I stretched our legs and took in the street view. I always thought that big red flying horse at some of the gas stations was a dandy.

Daddy came out of the station with two big bags of potato chips. Another treat since Mama said they were too expensive for what you get. I got busy crunching my chips and drinking another soda.

It was late, way past supper time. Mama had bananas, so we ate those to tide us over until we stopped again.

When we did stop, we ate at a diner. Another treat! It was empty except for a couple of guys sitting at the counter drinking coffee. Each man gave the waitress a thermos to fill up while they sat. They didn't appear to have eaten anything.

We got a booth. Daddy nodded at the guys as we walked by them.

"Truckers. Those boys got a tough job. Trying to get the beeves to market without any dying on the way. Gone from home over half the time. Missing their kids growing up. They get as many divorces as rodeo cowboys do."

He looked at the menu a minute and said. "Whatcha think, Mama? Is chicken fried steak tickling your taste buds?"

"These greasy spoon joints got some of the best of those steaks that can be found. You want to chance it?"

Mama nudged me with her elbow. "How 'bout you, Wes? You wanna split one with me, double order of potatoes and gravy?"

"Yes Ma'am, I sure do!"

Daddy was rubbing his chin stubble and thinking. "I just want the steak. I'll give Wes my potatoes. Too much starch will make me sleepy. I learned that in my long-haul driving rodeo days. I drank a lot of Cokes and coffee, ate protein, mostly in the form of a whole package of bologna, and only stopped for gas, the outhouse and to give my horse water and walk her around so she didn't road founder."

I think he was happy and full of sweet expectations for us. And, rightly proud he wasn't a trucker or a rodeo cowboy! My dad was a real cowboy. He grew up in the ranch life. He wasn't just a guy with a hat, he had a handle on the cattle! He stood six foot tall in his prime. He was muscular with broad shoulders and not an ounce of fat. He was, according to Mama, "a handsome kinda guy. Rodeo life was put away soon after I was born. Daddy felt the family needed a more stable life as soon as possible. So now he is a cowhand and horse trainer. He's had experience in animal husbandry, working with breeding programs--cattle and horses.

As we rode along, sometimes in silence, I was thinking of things I wanted to ask about the ranch, the town, whatever. Thoughts would come to my mind like a cap pistol shot or firecracker popping into my thinking. I was filled with all the expectation and curiosity a kid like me could have.

Mama began telling me the story of making this move: "Mr. McCleary offered Daddy the job after a 45-minute phone conversation. He accepted on the spot."

"I had a peaceful feeling about Mr. Mac and the Mesquite ranch."

"Of course, you did! And the salary they offered was such a big step-up from what we have been living on. This offer is too good to pass up."

"Mr. Mac had heard your Daddy was a good top hand. When he was asking around among the ranching community, Daddy got high praise many times. People said he was an expert horse trainer and knew his way around cattle."

"Many of them also spoke highly of his integrity. That means he is a man who can be trusted. The ranching business can be a small world and a person's reputation follows him. Mr. Mac said nobody had anything bad to say about Wes Redmond."

"The nearest town, Roca Grande (means "Big Rock" in English) is 18 miles from the ranch. It's a typical small Texas town. We will shop there most of the time, for groceries and other things not available at the Mercantile on the ranch. There's a town square that has a diner and coffee shop called Sally's Place, a movie theater, City Hall, a Five & Dime store, clothing and shoe store, hardware store, the Sheriff's office, doctors and dentist—I don't know what all! And Mr. Mac said Big Mike's Grill perfumes the air with barbecue scent all over town every day but Sunday!"

Daddy chimed in. "I was impressed with all that. It sounded like an ideal little Texas town. And, not too far from the ranch, which is off the beaten path."

"And with Big Mike's Grill, Mama can have barbecued brisket all the time!"

Mama and Daddy laughed. Only I wasn't making a joke. Oh, boy! Sometimes I just didn't get what the adults were about.

"Mr. Mac told me people from the ranch mingled with the people of Roca. The older ranch kids go to High School in town. Now, go on, Mama--tell Wes about the village and such on the ranch."

"Well, Mr. Mac said the little ranch village was built as part of the employee benefits. The employees pay no rent or upkeep. He said housing was figured out with a man's status and the size of his family."

"Each person and each family has value and respect. The ranch is not a commune where everybody is equal. He looks at a person's skill and ability, trustworthiness, how they get along with other folks."

Daddy added, "I think they don't want us to be just neighbors in the ranch community, they want us to be like a big family. He talked about the marriages among the people that make two families into one."

Chapter 2

"The McCleary's bought the ranch 25 years ago. The owners were elderly, and their children had no interest in ranching. The only housing was the bunkhouse. The few married hands rented houses in Roca. The McCleary's began to build houses for them. In time, they also built up the cowherd. This led to more cowhands hired, and younger cowboys marrying because they had a place to live. They also did a makeover on the bunkhouse, adding more room--built it bigger and better."

Mama added, "It sounds to me like the community grew one family at a time, one cowboy at a time, one house at a time. It began to take shape and is now a thriving little village. Mr. Mac allowed that most of the time it's happy and peaceful. It took a couple of years for the word to get around. Then, people started coming on their own, looking for a job at the ranch."

Daddy nodded, "He also told me there's enough people to do the work, so nobody has to work themselves into the ground. My workweek is five days. I have

Saturday and Sunday off. The bunkhouse hands take turns caring for the animals on weekends."

Mama smiled. "Mr. Mac said there's a waiting list for people who want to go to work on this ranch. But a lot of new hires lately are young people who were born and raised on the ranch."

Daddy was looking at the roadside. "I think we are getting close to our turn. The gate is tall and wide and has a welded iron sign up above that says the name. And, there it is right there!"

The sign said Mesquite Creek Ranch, but this place looked like the middle of Nowhere, Texas. We turned onto the dirt road that took us into the confines of this vast cattle ranch. Daddy drove slowly for several more miles. (It was just two, seemed like more!)

This pasture was cleared of brush and abounded with grass that looked about knee high on a grown man. There were no horses or cows we could see. A few rabbits galloped across in front of us. I saw quite a few birds like sparrows and little finches fluttering around. A covey of quail flew up, and there was a Road Runner who gave us a bit of a race, running beside the truck.

"Wes, look, here's some Mesquites right here by the road along that fence line. Aren't they great? I like the Mesquites."

What a memory this is for me. The trees I saw were very tall. Their trunks were gnarled, with tough looking bark. I hadn't seen much trees of any kind. All my life had been on ranches in the Panhandle north of Amarillo or the Oklahoma Panhandle, where the land was more like Kansas than most of Texas. That land is flat with no trees in any direction as far as you could see. I was highly impressed with the rugged and stately Mesquites. And later the oaks and pecans along the creek and riverbanks.

"You know, Daddy, I'm thinking I like the Mesquites, too." He looked over at me, smiling, and said, "I'm glad, Son."

As we drove into our new hometown, the dirt road became a street made with bricks. I thought the town looked like it was right out of a western movie. The buildings were made of clapboard siding and the sidewalks were boardwalks.

Rough log rails on the street side of the boardwalk were held up by posts in the ground, but there were no horses hitched. Just bicycles. Cars, trucks, and horses are not allowed on Main Street, that way the bricks stay clean.

The storefronts had big display windows. There was a General Store with large inviting windows that displayed merchandise. A beauty salon and barbershop shared a space, with a center curtain for dividing the room. The social hall called *Wet Your Whistle* was for grownups mostly. The kids and teens had The Soda Shop, which had comic books, board games, and a juke box.

Not too far off was the two-story schoolhouse. It was made with bricks like the ones paving Main Street. The park with swings was shaded by Oak, Pecan and Mesquite trees. It had picnic tables and a pavilion with a big dance platform. And, nearby, the centerpiece of town life: the church house, made with white cinder blocks. A sign in front of the humble building announced its purpose: It said simply: "Church Meets Here."

The houses were of various sizes set wide apart from each other. Each had a front porch going all the way across and dressed up by a wooden porch swing. There were garden plots, chicken sheds, and dirt streets winding around the houses. Out a ways, I saw a big water tower. Behind the stores opposite from the neighborhood, was a big building. It was not tall, but wide and long, like a low built barn.

"What is that big building, Daddy?"

"The bunkhouse, where the bachelor cowboys live. It reminds me of an army barracks. Huh! I see the bunkhouse and all the homes seem to have Swamp Coolers. The businesses, too, I expect."

These coolers were perfect for this area of Texas which is almost always dry in summer. These coolers work well in low humidity. A metal blower wheel turns inside pushing moistened air into the house. Water flows into cellulose on the inside of the metal unit. There is a water reservoir on the bottom. It cools amazing well.

Mama observed. "This is kind of a rarity. Most of the time, the luxury of a Swamp Cooler is not for ranch hand families. I grew up with a cooler. This is going to be a nice addition to the comfort of our new home."

This remote outpost would not be everybody's cup of tea, but Mama, and especially Daddy, were determined almost immediately that this ranch was HOME!

Mama took out her compact. She opened it and looked at her reflection. She dabbed powder on her nose and cheeks. Next, she found her lipstick, a light pink color. She checked her teeth, then applied the color perfectly to her lips.

Daddy drove slowly so we could take things in. Away from the houses were a few barns with corrals. Daddy said these held the milk cows owned by individuals, "kid" horses, and pens in a covered barn for the 4-H kids to keep the show animals. There was an arena for exercising them and a large pasture providing a place for the animals to run free and graze. Mr. Mac believed animals were not meant to be in small pens for hours on end. They needed time to be free in nature.

Dogs were everywhere--running after their kid owners, barking their greetings to the newcomers, chasing each other. There were people (mostly ladies and kids) around on the boardwalk. They turned to see us. They were smiling and waving. I waved back.

Some of the kids ran or rode their bicycles beside the truck. Some were shouting to us. I couldn't make out what they were saying, but their excitement was contagious! It was an idyllic scene, very welcoming.

I was decked out in my blue and white striped tee shirt, brand new jeans, and my new canvas sneakers. From what I saw of the other boys, I fit right in. I was at the beginning of a great new adventure.

I had a normal (for me) hard time meeting new people. But I didn't have that strange new kid feeling here. I had peace. I sat forward in the seat between Mama and Daddy to get a better look at what was going on.

"You know, Betty, I'm getting a feel for this place already. I think this is gonna be a great little town for the Redmond's to build our nest. I think the Lord has led us here, and we will put our roots down deep."

I felt a lot like what Daddy was saying. It almost seemed like I belonged here already.

Mama smiled a bit weakly. "I sure hope so, Duke."

He grinned and said, "Betsy, if you don't fall in love with this place, I'll eat my hat!"

She laughed at that. His good nature was hard to resist.

My Mama was no stranger to moving. When Daddy took this job, she said, "Well, I'm certainly tired of us living like Gypsies." She seemed to get more on board as we were driving and talking about it. But seeing it now, she seemed nervous about it again.

I had known for a while that Mama was unhappy. For a couple of months now she had been so sad. I heard her crying in her room sometimes. I wanted to comfort her. But when I asked Daddy about it, he shook his head.

"Let her figure it out by herself. Love her. Ask her to check over your homework or make you a sandwich. Show her you need her. And thank her for all she is doing for you. Hug and kiss her a lot. Be cheerful."

So today I chirped, "It's going to be fun for us, Mama. You get to meet new neighbor ladies. And help me figure things out at my new school. It's gonna be great, isn't it, Daddy?"

"Yes, it is, Wesley Boy. It is going to be super-duper!"

We came to a building that had a sign in big letters on the glass front door: "BANK." Daddy stopped the truck. "This is where Mr. McCleary is waiting for us."

In the bank, we were greeted by a man and woman. "Hello, you must be the Redmond's! Welcome to Mesquite Creek Ranch. I'm Tim Jones. This is my wife, Alice. We hope you will feel welcome here in our little community."

Mr. Tim had a big white straw hat which he removed when introducing himself. He had a thick head of brown hair. He sported a neatly trimmed, brown mustache. Mama said later those kind were called a "push broom mustache" like brooms the janitors at school used. It almost covers his mouth, but when he smiled, he flashed some beautiful pearly whites! He wore a wide leather belt with a silver rodeo trophy buckle. That surely caught my eye! His plaid western shirt was starched and ironed, like Mama did Daddy's. He had on Wrangler blue jeans. His dark brown boots were polished and shining. His face was kind, and his smile made me feel good. Mr. Tim shook our hands--even mine!

Daddy said, "Have we met before, Tim, you looked familiar to me?"

Tim laughed. "Well, I think it is possible that you saw me when I was active in rodeo. I was quitting about the time you got started, so we were likely at a few shows at the same time. You know, I thought I was hot stuff, so I probably passed you by. But later, after I broke my right shoulder, I followed your run. I was a fan. So, you look very familiar to me, too."

Miss Alice was pencil thin, with beautiful long blonde hair. She had a comb on each side above her ear for holding back the flowing locks. She was wearing a bright green cotton dress with a big white collar. Her skin was pale with light freckles under her makeup and more visible on her arms. She was wearing face powder, eye makeup, and red lipstick.

Mama was a Plain Jane compared to her. Later on, Miss Alice showed Mama how to apply some color to her face and mascara on her eyelashes. Daddy and I both thought Mama was pretty already, but the makeup made her stunning!

Miss Alice went over to Mama. "Hi, Betty, welcome!" She gave Mama a quick hug and patted her back. Then she looked at me.

"Well now, you must be Wesley! I'm thinking you might be interested in the soda shop across the street. I know you've been on the road all night. Besides sodas and ice cream, they have sandwiches, hot dogs, and hamburgers. You okay with that?"

"You bet, Miss Alice! I'm about starving right now!"

Chapter 3

We left the men behind to talk business. The Soda Shop is a great place. The teenagers were there visiting with each other--playing the jukebox and dancing. Younger kids were spending their allowance on ice cream and comic books. I saw them trading the comics around. I liked that idea and couldn't wait to get in on it!

We sat at the counter on those neat swivel stools. The young man behind the counter was looking spiffy in a red and white checkered shirt with a red bow tie. He also had one of those little oblong hats. Mama said he was called a soda jerk. His hair was so red it was orange! Thousands of freckles ALL over! He looked at me, winked, smiled big and turned to the ladies, "What can I get for you folks today?"

"Bring this young man whatever he wants that his Mama will allow. It's my treat today."

Mama nodded. "Go on, Wes, get what you want."

"Okay! I'll have two hot dogs with mustard, french fries, and, umm, a Coke Float."

Mama got water. Miss Alice ordered coffee. Then, she said, "Patrick, would you bring our order to that table?"

"Sure thing, Miss Allie."

We moved to the booth and Patrick was right there with their drinks.

Mama was looking at Miss Alice. "I got some questions."

"Aw, very direct. I like it! Fire away, Betty."

"First, should we call you Allie." "Of course! Everybody does!" We all laughed.

Mama fiddled nervously with her bracelet. Miss Allie lit a cigarette. It seemed like a tense moment, like something was wrong. All I wanted was my hot dogs, not adult problems!

"Well, I guess—I mean. . . I would like to know how the community works, and especially if this pleasant atmosphere today is sort of a show put on for us."

Miss Allie laughed. "I can see why you would want to ask that question. It almost seems too good to be true, doesn't it?"

Mama laughed, too, "Yes! It really does. All those kids on their bikes and running beside the pickup like they did. And everybody on the boardwalk waving to us made me wonder."

"Well, truly it is all for you, but it is purely spontaneous. We are a small community and very close knit. So, most everybody knew when you were coming and why. Nothing was planned. Whoever is around will welcome newcomers so they can blend right in."

I thought, I am going to have to start writing these words out for later, to ask Mama. What in the heck is spontownious?

She smiled and winked at Mama, "Duke is sort of a rodeo legend around here. We live a pretty low-key life. So, your family coming, Duke being a celebrity, is by all means--a stop-the-presses event!"

I didn't know what that meant either! But when Miss Allie and Mama laughed the way they did, I decided it must be okay that we stopped the presses.

Then, when my food came, there was a Moon Pie on the tray. I looked up quickly and Patrick put his finger to his lips in the "shush" position, then chuckled.

I was being very favorably impressed with my new hometown! And, Patrick was my new hero! I saw him at church that first Sunday we went. He spoke to me. "Hey, kid, how you doing?"

"I just moved here last week with my Mama and Daddy. I'm Wes Redmond." Patrick stuck his hand out and we shook. "Patrick McSwain, good to meet you, Wes. Yeah, I heard about your Daddy being a big rodeo champ. And your Mama is a one pretty lady. How do you like the ranch so far?"

"Huh!" I giggled. "Ever since you gave me a free Moon Pie at The Soda Shop, I have felt like this is home for me!"

"Good for you! So, I'll see you around, Wes."

Patrick was a rare teenager who had time for little kids. I learned he was an only child and liked to mingle with younger kids now and again.

I understood this. I paid attention to toddlers sometimes, too. I was longing for siblings. I could be a quiet sort of a kid. Being an only child played a part in that.

As I look back, I can see I was sort of bookish. I didn't think the way most of my peers did. I didn't think bathroom jokes were hilarious. What they thought was funny might make me very uncomfortable. . . especially if girls are around.

Maybe I was with grown-ups too much. I bonded closely with my parents. I admired my Daddy. I leaned on my Mama. And I loved them both! I had a tender heart and felt the pain of others. I also felt alone quite a bit, sort of like a misfit. All that began to change for me once I got to Mesquite Creek Ranch. I found out what it was to "belong."

Miss Allie went on about the ranch. "The McCleary's set the tone for life in the community. People being interviewed for jobs are checked out close. It's important that people are a fit for the atmosphere of the ranch. That way, not many who come here want to leave. Most who are not for this lifestyle change their mind about working here during the interview process. Some think they will like it, but after a while they miss the city sounds--we have no honking horns, no sirens, and no bad noisy drunken parties. We have peace."

Mama ordered a Coke Float. I could see her relaxing. She had stopped picking at her bracelet, twisting her rings, and swinging her foot under the table. Miss Allie was winning her over, and I was very glad of that.

Miss Allie got another coffee and lit up another cigarette.

"You know, Allie, I'm seeing this as a place where imperfect people try hard, fall down at times, and get back up again! And, there has to be structure and parameters in any society. The McCleary's want to have the right balance between freedom and being individuals. It's the ideal. But there will be times when that isn't how it goes. I think they know this and have a plan for how to get past the failures."

Miss Allie smiled. "Exactly. If we just throw people in here from all walks of life and ways of doing, it won't work. It will be like the world. But we are realistic enough to remind ourselves that Jesus hand-picked twelve men and even He got a rotten apple! So, we try to help people who want it. Mr. and Miss Mac don't give up easy."

"For some who don't seem to belong, it can be a place of second chances. We don't quit over a skint knee or a stubbed toe! There's a lot of forgiveness and do-overs before anyone is asked to leave. Mr. Mac says we can improve the things that might be a problem, starting with helping each other to get over our raising."

Mama slurped the last of her Coke Float and blotted her lips. "That is a great plan! Another thing that appeals to me is the idea of no wrong side of the tracks in the village. It is so refreshing. I also have an idea the remote location helps with the tight knit friendships here. Living cheek by jowl is a great way to keep us all on the straight and narrow."

Cheek by jowl? Straight and narrow? What is that?!! Another something I need to find out about. I was having a time keeping up with these "sayings."

"Betty, you're gonna love it here. I see you as a fine asset to the women here-- an example. And, it's a great place to raise children."

Miss Allie looked over at me as I shoved the last of my hot dog down and wiped mustard off my chin. She winked, but I saw a sadness in her eyes. I immediately thought—she doesn't have any kids. I wondered why that was, and how I somehow just knew it.

"You won't be surprised that Mr. Mac has a pet peeve about cursing. He considers it to be useless unless a man is fist-fightin' angry or hits his finger with a hammer." She giggled.

"Oh, Allie! I guess those are occasions a curse word could be overlooked. Duke says it is disrespectful to curse in the presence of ladies or children ever. And throwing impolite language into ordinary conversations offends people with a proper upbringing. It's best that a person never picks up the habit!"

"I think that's Mr. Mac's sentiment right there, Betty. He was raised Hard Shell Baptist--pretty strict. But he is an unusually tolerant man. He believes in letting folks find their way by following the example of those of us in leadership positions."

"There's no gambling outside in public. It's confined to homes and the bunkhouse. But there is dominoes and

Canasta at the Whistle. They serve beer limited to two bottles per customer. After that, there is bottled sodas and iced tea. No other alcohol is sold on the ranch. People are on their own with what they consume at home and off duty, but public drunkenness and/or disturbing the peace can be grounds for dismissal."

"Mr. Mac occasionally stops by the Whistle for a brewski with the folks. He says letting people see you being human is almost as important as them seeing you being holy. He makes appearances at The Soda Shop, too. He buys burgers, ice cream and sodas for all. The kids find him second only to Santa Claus!"

Mama and I were impressed by all this. "He seems to be dedicated to truly knowing the folks who call this place home and letting them know him. Is Miss Mac this open and involved?"

"Oh, yes. She is the Mother Hen of the ranch-- actively involved in what's going on. She and Mr. Mac work with Brother Harvey (our pastor) in counseling people from time to time--marriage troubles, money problems, and sassy-mouthed kids."

Miss Allie winked at me and grinned. I put my hand over my mouth and giggled.

"It really does sound like a family, Allie! Everybody is kinda looking out for the other, with the McCleary's leading the way. And people as diverse as a houseful of kids. Not a copy among them, every one of them a genuine original."

"So true. There is no right or room to judge another person harshly. We help people in whatever way we can. But, on the other hand, there is a definite ladder to climb among the people hired here. It has to do with leadership, skills and responsibility.

And, because Duke has all of those qualities, he gets a paycheck equal to that. It also means a bit nicer home. You and Duke got a great house--ready for move-in. There are two bedrooms, and if another child comes along, you'll be upgraded to three bedrooms and more square feet overall. Mr. Mac believes a man is worthy of his hire."

Mama nodded. As I listened, it seemed like the real thing to me. They were looking out for us, and not limited to only what Daddy can do for the ranch.

Miss Allie went on, "Tim and I will be helping with your unpacking unless you would prefer to do it by yourselves."

"Oh, yes, thank you! We're happy to have the help."

"Okay! And before I forget--there will be a church dinner to welcome you folks after the service next week. Tomorrow you'll need time to sleep in. You'll get more acquainted with folks at the fellowship dinner. Church attendance is not demanded at all, but it is encouraged."

At that moment, Daddy and Mr. Tim came in and joined us. I thought I had never seen my Daddy looking that happy. He slipped into the booth with me and Mama grinning from ear to ear.

"Well, we finished our welcome aboard session with Mr. Mac. What a great guy he is. A really pleasant man. Every step we take makes me feel that much better about moving here. We are going to be a part of something wonderful here."

Mr. Tim was sitting beside Miss Allie. He smiled under that mustache of his. "This is very true, God willing, and the creek don't rise! But right now, we need to get you folks set up in your new home!"

Daddy nodded and smiled. "Okay, you go on and get your pickup. Me, Wes and the ladies will walk on in that direction. You can follow us down the hill there toward the housing area."

As we walked, Miss Alice pointed to the first house right there in front on our right. "This is it, my friends, your new digs."

Daddy drove up beside us then and rolled along as we walked on up to the place we were going to call "home."

Chapter 4

All the houses were of simple frame construction--unpretentious and homey. Mr. Tim said they come in three sizes to accommodate family size. The floor plans are similar, and all houses are painted in one of these colors: pale blue, creamy beige, light yellow, pale green and white. Ours was a medium size. It was freshly painted white. A big clay pot of red Geraniums rested on the porch rail. The porch was all the way across the front of the house, stained rather than painted. It had an inviting wooden swing painted bright red. Nailed to the top rail of the porch enclosure was a sign, white with black letters: Redmond. Every house has a sign. It really helped when we first got here. Since there were no house numbers, no street names, the family name signs were a must.

Inside were tall windows in every room. The light streamed in. Only the west side had no windows. The living room was roomy, with leather furniture--a big couch, large size side chairs, and two small tables with matching white milk glass tam lamps. There was other pleasant décor, wood floors, and large oval braided rag rug. The kitchen floor was a pretty designed Mexican ceramic tile.

The master bedroom was large, and the closet was nice sized. Standing by the bedroom door was a fine built-in gun cabinet for storing Daddy's shotgun, rifle and ammo. It had drawers for storing gun cleaning supplies, hooks for hanging bird vests, binoculars and such.

There was a dresser with a mirror for primping and a small chair. A tall chest of drawers matched the dresser and the bed's headboard. We never had anything like that before—matching furniture! There was a cushy carpet almost to the walls on all sides of the master bedroom.

The bathroom was in the hall. It had a big closet for storing blankets, bedding, bath towels and so forth. The floor was the same Mexican tile we saw in the kitchen. In time we saw it around the ranch quite a bit, in various patterns and colors. The tub was modern--no feet, and it had a shower head!

My room had twin beds, a small desk, a three-drawer chest, and a wooden toy box with a lid. It already had a few new items waiting for me: a baseball mitt with a ball, a bag of marbles, a stuffed horse, a brand new toy six-shooter cap gun with belt and holster and several boxes of caps, a new Bobbsey Twins mystery book, a harmonica, and three new comics! My rug was a smaller version of the living room rug. I had a window where I could see our garden that was already planted for us with little shoots coming up.

My closet was adequate for my hanging clothes, with a low rod I could reach easily. I hung my coat and Sunday clothes on the hangers provided. It was the first "just mine" closet I ever had. I got my folded clothes into the chest of drawers. There was a small standing bookshelf in the closet beside the hanging clothes. It held my few books, my shoes, my sling shot, and odds and ends.

The toys I brought with me went into the chest with the new ones. My new toy horse rested on my already-made-up bed. I went back to the toy chest and got out the cap gun. I had never had one of these. I was over the moon happy with the toys and my room.

Mama was very pleased with everything, too. The kitchen had nice formica cabinet tops. It was open, fairly roomy. It had plenty of cabinet space, and a small pantry for spices, canned goods and storing extra items. The cook could see the family in the living room across the divider. On the dining table, resting on a small plate was a cluster of bananas.

There was a hall closet that housed winter coats and other items. The back-porch shelves had household items we might need right at first when there were boxes that might not be unpacked yet--bath towels, soap, toilet paper, and so forth.

Daddy and Mr. Tim brought in boxes labeled "WES" and "BD-RM" and "BATH-RM." They took them to the appropriate places. Ones like "SHOES" or "BOOKS" and "KNICK-KNACKS" were set against the living room wall for unpacking later.

Miss Allie jumped right in with the boxes labeled "KITCHEN." We didn't have that much, so it was quick work for her and Mama.

She pointed out their house, which was a bit back of ours. It was that pretty green color. "If you folks need anything, send Wesley over, and we will come running." She gave Mama a Roca Grande phone book and a little book for entering personal phone numbers.

She opened it and showed Mama where she had written under "J" -- Jones, Tim and Allie and their phone number. On the front page she had printed the mailing address of the ranch. It was a rural route number.

"We have big mailboxes at the highway. Mr. Carmichael, who runs the Mercantile is in charge of getting the mail and taking the outgoing mail every day. We all have boxes there in the store where he puts up our mail.

She looked at me and said, "You and Ozzie Carmichael may be in the same grade at school. He helps his Daddy in the store. He's an only child. He and his Daddy lost his Mama almost two years ago. She died very suddenly. You will probably meet him soon, I expect."

"That is real sad, Miss Allie. I hope to meet him. But I won't say anything about his Mama unless he does." She nodded.

Mr. Tim had left and now popped back in the front door with a big soup pot. "This here is beef stew Allie made yesterday for you folks to have later. It'll make a quick bite while you get settled and don't need to worry about cooking for a day or two." He put it in the refrigerator.

Daddy began thanking them for all the help they had been. "Betty and I have never lived anywhere that we got this kind of a welcome mat. I'm at a loss for words."

As they stepped out the door, Allie looked back. "Oh, Betty, I wanted to ask you something." She motioned for Mama to come out with them. They talked briefly. I could hear Mama chuckle and she hugged Miss Allie.

She came back in the house smiling. Daddy asked, "What was that about?" Mama kinda giggled. "Oh, you know--girl talk."

Daddy reached over and grabbed Mama, then he swung her around lifting her feet off the floor. We were all laughing. Sleep-deprived, road-weary, and hungry as horses, but we were so happy we could hardly contain what all the Lord had brought our way.

Then, there was a knock on the screen door.

As if on cue, three neighbor ladies came in carrying dishes that spoke to the senses of a hot meal. They told us their names. One announced, "We are here to welcome you." They stormed the kitchen, putting their food into our pots and pans.

The older of the three said, "Now, you won't have to worry about where to return our things."

The ladies looked like a mother and daughters. All of them were blonde, had on similar pullover shirts and pedal pusher pants. The older one was the "director." It was obvious they had done this before. They wasted no time with small talk.

They lit the oven. The fried chicken went into a baking pan covered with foil, then into the oven to warm up. They had green beans they put into our pot on a low flame, same with gravy. Potato chunks were still in hot water, put on a low flame so Mama could mash them at the right time. There was a big stack of warm flour tortillas, foil wrapped. And, a "just because" roomy paper bag with a couple of dozen homemade peanut butter cookies.

They set the table with folded paper napkins and our newly unpacked plates and silverware.

The mother asked, "If you don't mind, Mr. Redmond, you and Wes can help us carry out these pots and pans we brought over." We put their boxes into the car and took out four full paper bags. They gave us groceries!

My Mama was overwhelmed. She stood there on the porch like a statue. Daddy barely had time to call out "thank you" as they jumped in their car and took off. I waved and shouted, "Thank you!" They beeped their horn twice.

We came back into the house with the bags and set them on the table. Mama sat on the couch. I went over and sat beside her, holding her hand, as Daddy began to take things from the bags. He was being goofy, calling out each item one at a time.

"Well, what do we have here? A gallon of fresh milk, a big Mason jar of coffee, a package of bologna, a pound of flour, and a loaf of bread! Oh, looky here, Wes--your favorite breakfast. Corn Flakes! And, here's a dozen eggs, a bag of rice, a bag of pinto beans, a sack of potatoes, a sack of apples, five pounds of sugar, a pound of butter, a jar of Peter Pan peanut butter, and grape

Smuckers. And there are rolls of paper towels and two boxes of Kleenex tissues. Oh Boy! And right here on the bottom—a sack of chocolate kisses. Now, did you ever?!?"

Daddy was grinning. He went over to the couch, bent down, and gave Mama a big smoochy kiss. He sat down beside her.

I didn't understand what was going on. Why did all these strangers do all this for us? Mama was still sitting there, staring. Daddy stood up and said, "What a deal, Betty, isn't it?"

He put his hand out to help her up, but she looked up at him and busted out bawling. In that moment, something happened inside of her--deep in her soul.

I grabbed a box of tissues the people brought. She cried more for a bit, then dabbed her eyes and nose. "The rugs, the food, the quilts on the beds, and all the other things, all the furnishings, this house! These folks have given us gifts from the Lord. I can hardly believe it. I've never heard of anything like this in my whole life."

Daddy pulled her up from the couch and put his arms around her. They stood hugging each other for the longest time. He finally spoke, almost whispering, "New beginnings, my love. And yes, the good Lord surely is blessing us."

He told me a few days later that our Lord had taken away Mama's sorrow and given her hope.

Mama, ever the one for not wasting time, gave me a gentle elbow poke. "I believe we are going to make some friends here that will be for life. Especially, you! But right now, before we eat, we need to get these groceries put away."

We made quick work of that, and then surveyed the meal that was brought to us. There was a large platter of fried chicken, Cole Slaw, a pot of pinto beans, green beans, and homemade tortillas. For dessert--peanut butter cookies.

Daddy prayed that night as we sat down to eat. He thanked the Father for what was done for us already and what was to come for us in the days ahead. His voice cracked and he choked up, as he croaked out the "amen."

Chapter 5

We learned as time went on this welcome routine was exactly what it seemed to be—they did it every time a new family came to the ranch, and when there were newlyweds who moved into their first home. It's called "a pounding." Food donated by neighbors—a pound of this, a pound of that.

Mama went to get a shower. When she came back, she looked at me and said, "Wes, what do you think about taking a shower bath? Daddy can help you figure it out." In the first days of showers, we called it a shower bath to distinguish from a tub bath.

I got the hot and cold adjusted. Daddy showed me how to get in and secure the curtain before I turned the water up into the showerhead. There was no water splashing on the floor. I was already bathing and shampooing in the tub, so once I caught on to the shower routine, not getting the floor wet or water too hot, I was fine on my own.

I came into the living room in my PJ's. "My shower bath was great!" They both laughed, and Daddy said, "Maybe after this first one now, you shouldn't stay in quite so long. The hot water is all used up!"

I admitted that was why I got out when I did! We all laughed.

Then we said goodnight, and while Mama was getting me tucked in, Daddy did around with the dishes, scraping and rinsing with cold water. I fell into bed and was asleep immediately. We all slept way past daylight. I woke up lying under my brand-new handmade quilt Miss Allie left for me. I was still hugging my little stuffed horse. I could hear voices.

Daddy and Mama were in the kitchen, working on their last cups of coffee after breakfast. The day was well past getting up time.

"Well, there you are you sleepy head!" Mama got a glass of milk for me and fixed a bologna sandwich for my breakfast. Daddy went outside. Mama said, "He's looking over the garden and the shed. And I have already explored around inside a bit."

"I checked out the back porch. Our benefactors have it stocked with cleaning supplies. There's Bug spray for the garden. There's a shelf with canning jars. The back door opens on to the garden. It all seems handy as the pocket on your shirt!"

"What does benefactors mean, Mama."

"It means people who do things for others that is for that other person's benefit. It's a gift, so it doesn't cost the person anything!"

"Well, the people here surely did benefactor us. They thought of everything!"

"Yes, Honey, I think they did. Except for a washing machine--mysteriously missing. Now, a little further out back you will see there is a nice chicken house, surrounded by a big fenced yard for our hens to run around in. I hope you'll be my chicken man, Wes! You think?"

"Yes, ma'am! I am your chicken man, and so excited about learning how to take care of them. I have heard they can be mean, maybe peck you. Especially the roosters."

"Well, you know, your Daddy and I neither one have kept chickens. I guess we will all learn together as we go. I had a friend when I was a little older than you, and she had three pet hens. They all sat in her lap and liked to be petted. The neighbors will likely be a help to us with ours."

"Yes, Mama. That would be good. I saw chicken yards all over when we first got here to our house."

39

"Now then, I want to go over and ask Allie about a washing machine. And she wants to introduce us to a family right behind us. She said they are fine people. They have something she wants you to see. We can walk on over there when you finish eating and get your teeth brushed."

"Okay, Mama, I'm almost finished anyway."

She walked over to me, smoothed my hair, and kissed my forehead. Her hazel green eyes sparkled in the bright sunlight coming in the big tall window. She was so beautiful. And today, she looked more peaceful than I'd seen her in quite a while.

I didn't want to meet people so soon, but I told myself it needed to be done, so today was the day to get on with it. I didn't make friends easily. To tell the truth, I probably was on my way to being a loner. But that was about to change!

We walked toward the Jones house. "What is it Miss Allie wants me to see?"

Daddy smiled. "Just kind of a welcome surprise for us, I reckon."

As soon as we walked into their house and said good morning, Mama got down to business. "Allie, I was wondering about doing laundry. No washer and no clothesline either. Do we go into Roca to the laundromat?"

"I should have told you about that. It is quite a bit handier than driving to town! Over that way [she pointed] is our communal wash shed. It has twelve wringer washers, deep sinks for soaking, and lots of clotheslines out back of it."

"We actually enjoy our washing day, helping each other and catching up on the news. Every day is wash day, except Sunday. There's no schedule. Just catch as catch can. It seems to work."

Mama smiled. "Well, I shouldn't have worried about it at all, knowing this ranch has everything figured out! It sounds like a great set up."

"You get to where you look forward to it, every time I wash, I see different people there from last time. Now, today--we're going over to the Baker's to say hello. Their house is sort of next to yours, the blue one where the pickup has the hood up."

We went outside where Daddy and Mr. Tim were in their garden checking out the new plants shooting up-- soon to be food items.

The Baker's front door faced sideways and a little in front of our house. We could see the side of their porch, but not into the house. The houses were arranged so it

41

wasn't like a line of houses in a row. There's enough land for each home to have a space around it for gardens, chicken yards, tool sheds, garages. The houses can sit at angles to each other.

"The Bakers are T.J. and Irene. They have one child. Her name is Mary Lee. She's around your age, Wes. She's nine, I think."

I disliked the "meet the neighbors" thing. My parents continually conspired to find friends for me. I thought immediately this was what this visit was. I wanted to go at my own pace, take my time finding out who my friends were going to be. And certainly, none of them would be girls! Yecch!

Chapter 6

But, Hey! Hold the phone, Leroy! And, whadda-yuh-know?! I liked Mary Lee Baker instantly! She was so pretty with her dark brown--reddish highlights--braided hair and a sweet smile. She had pale skin.

It was that "china doll" look that became much loved by me as time went by. Mama told me Mary Lee's skin was like alabaster, which is a very white mineral rock that was carved into statues a long time ago in the days of Ancient Greece. I came to like that fancy word.

That day she was wearing a bright blue spring dress that made her vibrant eyes look super dark blue. And they were framed by some gorgeous long dark eyelashes. Blue bows were tied to her braids. Her shoes were black patent leather with a strap across the top of her dainty little foot.

She seemed too dressed up, like for church. I learned later that her Mama had her fixed up that way most of the time. She was an only child. Her Mama seemed overly protective of her one little chick.

Mary Lee had a doll she loved dearly. In time I saw the doll was wearing an outfit that matched her clothes quite a lot of the time. Miss Baker was a seamstress like Mama.

That first day, while the adults all talked in the house, Mary Lee and I were on the front porch. She asked me if I wanted to hold her doll. Timidly, she offered, "Her name is Peggy."

I didn't actually want to hold her doll. But I didn't want to hurt her feelings. I decided I would hold the doll for a minute. I even tied the bow on her bonnet which had come undone. Mary Lee was thrilled that I did that.

"You are so nice, Wes. You are my friend now," she cooed. She flashed a shy smile, "Thank you for holding Peggy." She took Peggy back. I just smiled a goofy grin like a stupid-dumb-struck-boy.

Mrs. Baker appeared. "Mary Lee, let's show Wesley our surprise." She clapped her hands and laughed. We all went out to their shed. There, in a corner was a big cardboard box containing five squirming, squeaking little puppies.

I held and petted each one. They were so cute with their little floppy hound ears. My Daddy walked over closer to me. He squatted down beside me. "Wes, the Bakers want you to have one of these pups for your own. What would you say to that?"

My heart almost stopped. Then it started to pound. I had been begging for a dog longer than I had a memory. But we were never settled enough or didn't have a place where it was possible to have one. Now, here at the ranch, it's like an unwritten law or Code of the West that every family had at least one dog!

"Which one do you think is yours, Wes?" Mary Lee was eager to see who I would pick. The pups were slick-haired, mostly reddish-brown with a black muzzle. They all had white on the chest, stomach, paws, and the tips of their tails. I saw one with a balance of the colors and a white flash between its eyes.

I made my decision quickly. "This one. This is the one I want."

She was thrilled. "That one is my favorite, Wes!"

The little thing was a beauty. I held her close. She licked my chin and I could smell her puppy breath. I carried her home in a shoebox provided by Mrs. Baker. The Bakers gave us puppy food to tide us over until we got into town.

Standing on the porch, Mr. T.J. began to tell me the rules of dog ownership. He was a big man like Daddy, almost scary to a half pint like me.

"Wes, having a dog means you will take care of her—food, fresh water, and cleaning up after her. You know, Poop Patrol." He grinned and I laughed. I liked him already. He said "poop." A word Mama didn't like me to say. She thought doo-doo was better.

"But each of us is also responsible for our village. So, if you see dog poop another dog owner missed, you clean it up! You got that?"

I nodded heartily, kind of gulped and finally said, "Yes, Sir, I got it!"

"Okay then! I understand you have never had a dog before."

"No, Sir. But I have always wanted one almost before I was born!"

Everybody laughed at my hyperbole.

"Well, Son, as a life-long dog lover myself, I can tell you there is not a better companion animal and friend than a dog. Human friends will let you down at times, hurt your feelings, but a dog will never say anything to hurt you or make you cry! They won't say a word against you." Mr. T.J. chuckled.

We laughed again. "A word against you." Dogs can't talk at all! He made a funny.

"It may sound kind of harsh with the rules we have around the ranch, dog doings being just one. But to keep the people and animals on this ranch going and doing, there must be understood ways of making it work."

"Yes, Sir, I understand. Mama told me that rules are important for a family, a classroom and even a town to keep things going."

"Well, now your Mama is a smart lady. And, you're learning right from wrong."

"I know! Mama says we can't just do whatever we want any time we want to. So I am a real rule keeper! I will be on the job with poop patrol, for sure!'"

"A lot of truth in your Mama's words." He smiled and stepped off the porch, reaching out for a handshake. When I looked at his hand, I saw a giant silver ring with a big square blue-green stone on the top. Impressive.

I felt relaxed and like Mr. T.J. was my friend now. I thought it wouldn't be rude to ask about his ring. "I like your ring, Sir. It's cool. What kind of a ring is it?"

Mr. T.J. smiled and said, "Thanks, Wes. This ring belonged to my granddaddy. When he passed away, it was given to me, the oldest grandson. Grandpa wore it at all times. The stone is turquoise, a favorite gemstone of Indians. My family on my Mama's side are Oklahoma Chickasaw Indian."

I sucked in my breath. "Then you are a real Indian! Wow!"

Mr. T.J. laughed, "Yes, I sure am! I'm a registered Citizen of the Chickasaw Nation. There are several of us here on the ranch. Some of the best cowboys you will ever see are Indians. Nobody sits a horse quite like we do!"

He winked at me and grinned.

Mary Lee followed us down the steps. She was sort of wringing her hands. I wondered if she was nervous. She smoothed her hair on top of her head. I really liked her braids.

"Goodbye, Wes. I'm so happy to have you for my new friend. Please come back and see me."

I turned around. "Bye, Mary Lee. I'm glad I met you, too. And thank you so much for giving me this puppy. I will love her and take good care of her."

And then I thought to myself, you don't need to worry about me coming back to see you, Miss Mary Lee, 'cause I will!

I didn't quite know it then, but I was smitten by the little princess with the dark blue eyes and reddish-brown braids. Really. . . Hopelessly. . . Smitten!

When we got home, Mama and I went looking among the moving boxes we had just emptied. She found the right size my pup could use as a bed. Mama got an old plaid flannel work shirt of Daddy's out of her rag bag. It had a torn sleeve. Mama cut it off at the arm hole so the puppy couldn't get caught in it. She threw in an old bath towel she had saved to put with the cleaning rags. We put those into the puppy's box.

I was rubbing the pup's stomach. I remarked to Mama about how beautiful Mary Lee was. Mama nodded, "She is a very pretty little girl, Wes."

I told her I was really impressed with her shoes. "Oh, my yes, Son, those shoes are classic. I wore them when I was a little girl, too. They're called Mary Janes."

"You know, you have an eye for fashion, Wes. Some say shoes make the man or the woman! A wrong choice in shoes can ruin the look of a quality outfit. Even old shoes need to be cleaned and polished."

I can't remember when I didn't know it was Mama's job to teach me. Because of her way of looking at things, I've had a lifelong care for my appearance--my shoes, my hair, and my clean fingernails. It isn't an ego thing for

49

me. It is just a protocol of being squared away and having a care for looking good inside and out.

Mama said, "If a person doesn't have respect for how he looks, other people may decide they shouldn't respect him either."

I nodded my understanding. "Well, Mama, I have to admit I liked Mary Lee's Mary Jane shoes. They look like doll shoes, and she looks like a doll, too. I mostly liked everything about her. She is a sweet person and beautiful, too." Mama stared at me for a minute but turned and said nothing. I thought she was about to speak, but she didn't.

My puppy slept with me every night from the first night on. I had found myself a canine friend to go along with my new human friend. It was a fine day!

Two or three times each night my little dog woke me up to go outside. This was a pattern for quite a while until she got better control. I took her outside often, so, very few "accidents."

I puzzled over a name for my baby dog. I remembered hearing Mama say some time ago, "The mercy of God is new every morning." I thought about my dog, waking up every morning so glad to see me. I knew mercy is a gift from God, so---she is "Mercy."

Before I went to bed, that first night, I got out my Big Chief tablet and wrote this:

> *Deer Mr an Miss an Maryley Baker*
> *Thank you four givin me Mercie.*
> *I will love her awl my life.*
> *Yours turley,*
> *Wesley H. Redmond*

I got under the covers holding Mercy, I thanked the Lord Jesus for this gift, and my new life here on this ranch. Then, for my new friend. She was the first classmate I met since I got here. I felt like that made her special. Little did I know just how special she really was.

Chapter 7

Daddy didn't go to work right away. He needed time to get us settled. People were so friendly, but we still needed to mentally process and take in our new surroundings. Mama seemed especially out of her element. He helped her with small things--like hanging pictures. They took walks around the neighborhood introducing themselves to folks out in their yards.

The day after I got Mercy, I ate breakfast and asked Mama if I could go check out the neighborhood.

"Sure! I know you want to show off Mercy and make some friends, so get outta here!" I laughed, grabbed up my pup, and ran out the door. I had my thank you note in my jeans pocket.

The day was nice and warm, sunny too. I went straight over to Mary Lee's house. She was on the front porch when I got there. She was dressed up again. Her shoes were more casual. They were sandals. I kept looking at them, sandals and feet. She had her legs crossed in front of her with knees bent and pointing to the sides.

When she stood up for us to get in the swing, I got a look at both feet and shoes. Her feet were perfect--small and evenly matched, no toes great bigger than the others. This girl was really gorgeous from tip to toe and back.

Her blouse was white with green buttons down the front. Her gathered skirt was green like the buttons. She and Peggy were dressed alike again. But her hair was different. It was curled in long ringlets bouncing beside her cheeks and down her back. I didn't like it so much. I preferred the braids.

She seemed glad to see me, and I was happy to see her. We sat in the swing and on the porch steps. She had her doll and I had my dog.

Their dog actually belonged to Mr. T.J. Before she got puppies, she went riding in his pickup most every day. When her puppies were gone, she went to the vet to get "fixed" so she wouldn't have any more. Then in a few days, she was Mr. T.J.'s sidekick again.

Miss Baker (Irene) brought us some lemonade and cookies. I gave her the note. She read it and smiled. "You are very welcome, Wes."

Mary Lee and I talked about school, my dog, and kid stuff around the neighborhood. I was mystified, captivated, and charmed by this girl.

But soon I could see that she talked like a young child, maybe five years old. I didn't know what to make of that. It didn't seem right.

In our conversation that day, Mary Lee said, "I don't go to school. Mama teaches me at home." I didn't ask why. It was important, but maybe impolite to ask about it. In that day, nobody had ever heard of "home-schooled."

After a while of swinging and the cookie timeout, I noticed a boy walking toward us. He was wearing a big ol' grin. "Who is this kid walking' up?" She turned her head, "Oh, that's Burley. He's my friend, too."

Burley was the opposite of me in looks. I was skinny, had straight dark hair, brown eyes, and I was kind of small for my age.

He was tall and husky, with curly-ish blond hair and blue eyes. We both had a Flat Top haircut, though. It was the rage!

He looked straight at me, still grinning. "HI, Mary Lee. Who's the new guy?"

She giggled but said nothing. I was pretty sure he knew who I was.

"I'm Wesley Redmond. I go by Wes. Just moved in here with my folks a couple of days ago. This here is my dog, Mercy. The Baker's gave her to me."

"Well, now, pleased to meet you, Wes and Mercy. I am Burley Whitfield. I'm ten years old, and I am big for my age." Then he laughed, and Mary Lee and I laughed, too.

Burley had that guileless honesty about him that just made you like him. What you see is what you get.

I thought "Burley" was a nickname because I thought it meant big guy or tough, something like that. And since he was big built and tall, it seemed to fit. I found out later his given name is Burleson, which is his Mama's maiden name.

I had always covered my introverted personality, which I get from my Daddy, by forcing myself to be friendly and outgoing like Mama. Only, I talk more than she does.

Daddy says, "Wes could get in a conversation with a fence post!"

My new friend Burley was happy among larger numbers and just two or three people, it didn't matter. I loved the company of others but not in the bigger numbers that Burley was good with.

In time we learned to flow with each other in both situations. He could over-shadow me and I didn't mind. In my bookworm world, I was very much his equal and sometimes advisor. It was a good plan.

Burley already knew about the puppies, of course. He told me I picked the prettiest one in the litter. He held Mercy, petted her gently with his almost man-sized hands. As we talked Mary Lee mostly listened.

"You and I will be in the same class at school because it's a small school. Each teacher has two grades at a time. There's a teacher for first and second grade, and so on. The teachers are all wives of men who work here at the ranch. But, 9th grade is alone because they are getting ready to go to High School."

"Mr. and Mrs. Mac have a test the teachers take before they are hired. Some of them have been to college. Our 5th and 6th grade teacher is their daughter, Audrey. She was Valedictorian in her graduating class. My Daddy says our school is as good, maybe better, than ones my brothers and sisters went to before we came to the ranch."

"How long have you lived on the ranch, Burley?" He blinked and said brightly. "I was born in Roca Grande hospital, but I was livin' right out here two days later."

"Wow! I have lived on so many ranches, I don't remember. It seems like you have a real home here. I want that, too. I want friends that I can keep my whole life."

He stared at me for a minute, kind of strange. Then, he blurted out, "So, Wes, do you believe in Jesus?"

Looking back, it doesn't seem like a topic kids our age would bring up. We didn't even know each other. But it didn't seem weird at all that day.

I answered quickly, "Yes, I surely do believe in Jesus! My Daddy says our family isn't the kind who goes to church every time the door opens, but we live our lives praying and trusting Him to help us with our problems."

"And, so I guess you believe in Him, too?"

Burley laughed that great big hearty laugh I came to love. "Are you kidding? I was practically born in church. My granddaddy is a preacher. I do love Jesus!""

He paused, looked thoughtful, then smiled again.

"Wes, you and I are gonna be best friends. Heck, we're gonna be like brothers."

I felt terrific about being Burley's friend. And, it was not lost on me that he had said we were going to be brothers. At that time, I wanted friends almost as bad as I wanted siblings. He might work for both!

I remembered a time when I asked Mama about getting a brother or sister, but I could see it wasn't something she wanted to talk about it. She was not upset at me for asking, but I felt like it upset her that I did.

I asked Daddy. "Well, Wes, that subject there is . . .uh, it's, ah, well, sort of complicated. One of those things that we--you and me and Mama have to wait on God for getting' us another baby."

"The Bible says He is the one who gives the woman a baby. So your Mama and me quit asking Him about it. We figure we should trust Him for what we need. We love you, and we are happy with just you."

I didn't understand all of it, but I thought it might be about waiting to see what God did or didn't do and being happy while you waited. I wanted a brother or sister, but for now, Burley was saying we're going to be brothers! I thought maybe that meant he was all I needed.

While Burley was talking, Mary Lee was smiling as usual. She said, "I love Jesus." She seemed almost angelic to me, very pure in heart.

Mrs. Baker came outside to check on us. "Miss Irene can Mary Lee go with us for Wes to see Mesquite Creek?"

It was a spring-fed creek that ran for miles through the ranch, providing water for all. And Burley said it had a wonderful swimming hole.

"Yes, she can go, but you kids can't dawdle long. It's getting close to lunchtime. And, you keep a close eye on her, Burley."

She stared at him. "Oh, yes, ma'am, I surely will."

Then she turned to Mary Lee. "Come in the house and change into your jeans and sneakers."

In a flash, we took off out of the housing area running toward a stand of big Mesquite trees off in the distance. None of us were much runners, so we slowed down to a walk.

I asked an important question. "Are there any rattlesnakes there around the creek?"

Burley shook his head. "No, we see all kinds of critters down there at times, mostly like coons, armadillos and possums, or maybe a skunk. Sometimes we surprise deer that are getting a drink."

"Mr. McCleary says the rattlers were killed out down there a long time ago. Early every spring when the snakes come out from hibernating the cowboys go down to the creek to the spot where we fish and swim to make sure it's safe. Nobody has ever been snake bit at the creek that I ever heard of."

"I am sure glad to hear that. I have no love for snakes. Gives me the willies."

He chuckled. "Me too, Wes-man, me too."

As we walked along, we heard voices. The ground began to slope down. We could see the treetops and then their trunks and the creek. Now I could see the kids and the swimming hole.

Burley said some of them were fishing or maybe skipping rocks. Probably the water was too cool for swimming. Mary Lee went over to where the girls were sitting together. Burley and I walked over to the guys. We sat down where Burley had her in his line of sight.

Two guys were fishing, and some others were shooting marbles on a level spot they had cleared off for their game.

One of the boys said, "Hey, Burley. Who's the gimp?"

Burley frowned and said in a flat tone of voice, "This here is my new friend, Wes. And you're gonna tell him who you are and how sorry you are for your big fat mouth."

The kid's eyes got wide as he stared at Burley. He ducked his head down. "I'm Jimmy Snyder, Wes, and I'm real sorry for what I said and happy to meet you."

I stood there confused, not knowing what had just happened.

Burley said. "Now then, isn't that all better?"

Then, things went on with chewing the fat, shooting marbles, and all the kids admiring Mercy and playing with her. Other dogs came over to make her acquaintance, with a sniff or two.

She had taken a long nap at the Bakers and was ready to play. She barked at the big dogs and toddled along after them. They almost seemed to laugh at her. I did, too. She was big stuff to be such a runt at the moment.

I had seen the creek and the swimming hole now. I pictured some great times in summer there. We started up the hill, with me thinking this was a fun start to getting to know the ranch and the other kids.

I hadn't known what to expect, and this was better than I had thought it would be.

Burley wanted to make sure I was okay. "Jimmy is new to the ranch, too, Wes. Some kids are rude and don't know they are. He's a good kid."

"He seemed fine to me. I didn't understand what it was he said anyway. I'm not mad at him or anything."

Chapter 8

I got home just in time to eat. Mama was getting the food on the table. I washed up and Daddy said grace. I thought of what had happened and said, "What does gimp mean?"

Daddy and Mama stopped with forks in mid-air. At first, they just looked at each other. Then Mama calmly said, "Why do you ask, Wes?"

I told them the whole thing--Jimmy's remark that led up to his apology at Burley's insistence. And that Burley seemed to think I had been insulted.

They both smiled. Daddy chuckled and said in a matter-of-fact way, "It's about your bum leg, Wes. People are just curious, and kids don't always have good manners about such things."

Mama added, "Your friend Burley sounds like a great guy. And, Jimmy, too."

I got my bad leg when I was a little kid, so I don't remember anything about it--just what they told me. It was broken in an accident when I was playing around in the barn. There was no money for a doctor. Daddy took me to the vet they used. They did an x-ray.

We talked on, Mama and Daddy asking questions about the swimming hole and what Burley had told me about school, and so on. It distracted me from the part about my leg, so it wasn't a problem. I guess because Daddy and Mama didn't make a big deal about it or act like it was a problem.

The break wasn't bad, so the vet helped make a splint for my leg. Mama kept me in bed for a good while.

They carried me back and forth to the dinner table, the toilet, the couch making sure I didn't put any weight on my leg. I don't remember any of this at all.

The result was a strong, healed leg that was a little "off." It made me sort of limp along. I could do anything other kids did, except ride horses. Mama told me later she was fearful I could be severely injured and come away crippled if I fell off a horse.

I was okay with that since horses are just so BIG. I was and still am, very afraid of them. Something I never told my Daddy. I was happy to keep my feet on the ground or peddling a bike.

I went on to tell Mama and Daddy about the size of the Mesquites at the creek. "They are huge! Like, ginormous! They were way, way over our heads, and bigger around than the fat man's waist at the circus."

Mama thought that was hilarious and laughed like crazy. We had been to the circus in Oklahoma City not long before we came to the ranch.

"Burley told me all about the dam the cowboys had built to make the swimming hole. And how the water goes on downstream, taking water to the other side of the ranch."

After we finished lunch I laid down for my mandatory nap. I almost always went to sleep no matter how I tried not to. Mercy was the best nap buddy in the world.

I woke up and went back outside and ran into a game of Cowboys and Indians. Sometimes the girls played with us. They were pioneer women. They brought rags to wrap our wounded heads and arms and pulled out imaginary arrows.

When Mary Lee played with us, I was always wounded multiple times. I would yell "Mary Lee!!!" She would come running to fix me. Oh, the drama of it all! And my love for her was growing every day.

Daddy spent the first week on the job being escorted around by Mr. Tim. They visited the bunkhouse several times so Daddy could see as many of the cowboys as possible, as they came and went. All meals went two hours to make sure every cowboy was fed.

They went to the blacksmith shop. Arthur Two Horses, was the blacksmith. Charlie Two Horses is his son. Mr. Art and Mr. T.J. are first cousins. His father and Mr. T'J.'s mother were brother and sister. Mr. Art was tall and even bigger built than Mr. T.J. He had muscles on top of his muscles.

I asked Daddy about that. He told me farriers work pretty hard with their hands and arms, so they have unusual strength there. Mr. Art kept the horses on their feet, literally.

Becoming friends with Charlie got me privileges to hang around the blacksmith shop with Charlie, Burley, and Ozzie. It was neat to watch Mr. Art work. Sometimes he had some chores for us. If a job he was doing was dangerous because of flying hot sparks from his hammer or when he welded, he would run us off.

One day I asked him some questions about bloodlines. "Mr. Art, I know Mr. T.J. is your cousin, so that does mean Mary Lee is a Chickasaw, like Charlie?"

He smiled. "Yes, that is true. She is a Chickasaw, for sure. She and her Daddy both have citizenship in the Chickasaw Nation. T.J. was the one who got me hired here. He drove to Oklahoma to help me move my family here. He's a good man."

For some reason that was a big deal to me. Mary Lee was an INDIAN. Her alabaster skin and red highlighted hair would have fooled anybody, but I was glad to know that she had a real American heritage.

Daddy told me more than once, "The Indians were here first, way before we were!"

Daddy and Mr. Tim rode for miles around the ranch. He gave Daddy a map that showed various large pastures where the cowherds and horses were rotated from one place to the other. Each cowboy had two or three favorite horses they rotated so they were not worked too hard. Each pasture's grass rested too, while the animals moved from one place to another. Daddy quizzed Tim about ranch life and the people who live and work here.

"Every ranch has its way of doing things, Wes. I gotta learn how Mr. Mac rolls with his men working here and his livestock."

Daddy liked to tell me about things, too. "You learn things by asking questions. Just have to make sure what you ask isn't a none-of-your-bees-wax question, like 'when did you stop cheatin' at cards?'."

He laughed and I did, too. Mama told me about some things it wasn't mannerly to ask. So, I understood what Daddy meant.

Chapter 9

Daddy learned how the single cowboys fit into ranch life with the families. Some of the younger cowboys miss home and the family life they left behind. Mrs. Mac felt it was an essential part of their happiness for them to be able to mingle with the families.

The church has a covered dish meal after services once a month. The cowboys are treated to various homemade dishes that bring them warm memories. They get a taste of home cooking like Mama made. Even some who couldn't manage to get up in time for service were welcome to squeeze in for the meal.

The cowboys have a comfy bunkhouse, with homey décor and much more room than the U.S. Army offers. The beds are longer and wider than a standard bunk, for accommodating the proverbial Long Tall Texan. Each bunk has a custom-made innerspring mattress.

They all have a clothing locker against the wall by their bunk and a footlocker at the foot. The living/dining/kitchen area is expansive and inviting. It is furnished with a couple of couches, and big easy chairs in the conversation areas. Round tables each seating six people for eating or playing cards.

The man hired to cook for the boys is called "Cookie." Among his talents, he was also "Doc" in a pinch. Some folks said he must have been a medic in the army. He is a whiz at patching up banged up cowboys, sewing cuts, but he knew when to say, "Get him to the hospital!" He is called on by the ranch families, too. He was a pretty good pediatrician.

I met Cookie at church soon after we got here. He grinned, "How you doing with fitting in here at the ranch, little Redmond?" I was caught off guard, but of course never at a loss for words!

"Well, Sir, I have friends already: Mary Lee Baker, Burley Whitfield, Ozzie Carmichael and Charlie Two Horses. I also got a puppy named Mercy, born right here on the ranch. I never had friends like these or any dog at all, until I got here. This ranch is the best place I have ever lived!"

"You know, kid, I feel the exact same way as you!!" He stuck his hand out for a shake and smiled big. "Any time you want to, Son, you and your friends stop by the bunkhouse, and I'll rustle up some grub for you, or at the least, sweet tea."

I liked Cookie right then. He was everything that Mesquite Creek Ranch is about. Me, Burley, Charlie and Ozzie would stop in every now and again to visit with him and see what was cooking.

The cowboys were always welcome at all church functions. The annual Christmas party was held in the big church hall. Every person employed on the ranch got a cash bonus--a months' wages. The children all got a small gift.

Some older cowboys had worked for years going from one place to another. The McCleary's made Mesquite Creek Ranch an oasis where drifters could stay put, misfits could find a place to belong, young men could marry, and couples had children. And, we all would live together in our little village where we put down roots, found a real home and lifelong friendships. Then, when a person's work was done, our cemetery "Boot Hill" would be the spot where we would find our final resting place on Earth. It is a cradle to the grave plan!

All employees had health insurance and Social Security. Mr. Mac also had a retirement plan of his own that was an upgrade: when someone couldn't work anymore, they could stay here, and be cared for by the ranch until their death. No matter what the problem might be, Mr. Mac and the neighbors would figure out what to do.

Sometimes there were problems in ranch society. Some of the younger cowhands tended to have an eye for the older high school girls. Mr. Mac had a strict policy about the bachelor boys getting chummy with under-age female "children."

Mrs. Mac formulated a plan that would improve on that hard rule. He saw the wisdom of it and gave his approval.

Mrs. Mac hosted a coffee klatch with mothers of teenage daughters. She presented her plan to them. Girls sixteen and older, with parents' permission, could tie a blue ribbon around their wrist. It signified they were available for dating, even the young cowboys who were under twenty years old. They discussed it, pro and con, kicked the idea around. Mrs. Mac assured that parents made their own rules about what their kids could do. They took a vote then, and it was Sweet Sixteen time for all. So, the plan to give the ranch girls a "coming out" went forward.

This blue ribbon on the wrist custom was put into practice a couple of years before my family arrived at the ranch. Mama was told all about it. When the plan went forward, the McCleary's oldest daughter Audrey, already seventeen, was wearing her blue ribbon the next day at school!

Audrey surely broke the ice there. They immediately began appearing here and there--at The Soda Shop, all church functions, and the parties at the pavilion-- cowboys and schoolboys were asking the girls with blue ribbons to dance.

The fellowship functions at the church building nourished the heart and soul of the village. Friendships were strengthened by us being together. People embraced and accepted one another.

Daddy, Mama, and I met with Brother John Harvey, right after we got to the ranch. He was a warm and welcoming man. We learned later he came from a family of preachers and missionaries. His mother died on the mission field in Korea after the war there was over. He was a widower with no kids, loved by all. He took care of all the people, saint and sinner alike, whether you came to church meetings or not.

He and Mr. Mac were the best of friends. Daddy said they have "a like precious faith," which is a line from the Bible.

Christmas and Easter Sunday were important days at the ranch. And the church was usually packed. My first Easter there was three weeks after we arrived. It was an exciting extravaganza. There was an egg hunt for the little kids and a spectacular meal with enough food for the whole town. The kids changed clothes so they could jump rope, hang out at the park, and play ball into the afternoon.

Each family brought covered dishes and desserts. The ranch provided the barbecue. The bunkhouse boys came early to set up tables and chairs on the dance platform, then stayed after for cleanup.

The pavilion provided shade, and if the stray rain shower wasn't pouring hard people could linger in conversation and stay dry. These parties could go on until the kids began to think about supper and lights out.

When we came to the ranch, both it and Roca Grande were in a kind of time warp that went back into the 1940's. A lot of the current fads and fashions passed by this part of the world. It was a simple life and time. Without television, there were no enticing ads to show us all the latest things we didn't have and didn't even know how desperately we needed them!

One day we were walking home from the monthly meal gathering, Mama said: "Each one of these parties seems to close with a happy sigh and a feeling that all is well in our little community." She was right, of course.

After the Easter break, it was time for school to start up. I was already acquainted with quite a few kids and had my two best friends. So, I didn't have my usual angst about going to a new school.

That first day, Mama was putting on her hat to go with me. I stepped out on the porch to wait for her. Burley was walking towards me, "Hi, Wes, you ready?"

"You bet I'm ready! This is gonna be a wonderful day for me!"

"Yes, it is! I know you will like school. The teachers are the berries. They either gave birth to us, are kin to us, are our neighbors, or gluttons for punishment, but either way, they love us!" He laughed at his glutton joke and made me laugh, too.

The church/school bell started ringing. It must have been audible for miles. I had already been to three schools in my young life, and none of them had a bell. I came to love that sound. It still reminds me what growing up in rural America was like.

Mama came out on the porch, and we all started walking to school.

We joined another lady and her son. They were going slow. Her boy was young, not walking fast. Must have been a first grader. The lady introduced herself.

"Nice to meet you, Mrs. Freidman. I'm Betty Redmond. We recently moved here. I was wondering about something that you might know. What sort of a music program does the school have? I haven't heard anything about that."

"Oh, please call me, Penny! Yes, well--they had a music teacher once, about three years ago. He was frustrated, thinking there was no way to get a music program going with only an old outta tune piano. Some parents said he was uppity and seemed to think of himself as better than us plain ol' country type people."

"Hmm. Sounds like a look-down-my-nose-at-you kind of a person."

"Right you are, Betty. My older boy was in the program and from what he told me; the children didn't warm up to the man much either. When he went to speak with Mr. Mac about doing something about the piano, he was so rude and demanding Mr. Mac fired him on the spot. Mrs. Mac was plenty upset. She wanted a music program. But the subject was never brought up again."

She grinned at Mama and said, "Until now!"

Mama was quick on the trigger, "Oh, no, you don't! I'm not volunteering for anything. I'm curious about what is going on with our school." But when we got into the building, Mama said, "Now where is that room with the piano?"

Miss Penny pointed. "There, end of the hall, on the left. That's the art and music room. The music teacher taught art, too, so there's no art now either."

My mind had wandered as we walked along. I thought of Mary Lee, not with us. It didn't seem right to me. She should be here. Only a few days had gone by since I met her, but she and Burley had taken on a great importance in my little world. The more I thought about Mary Lee missing out, the worse I felt. I was sad.

I thought to myself, "Wes, what is wrong here with you? This should be a happy day for you!"

I prayed, asking God to help me with a mess of emotions I was going through.

Chapter 10

[April 1952, 3rd grade, 8 years old]

Burley tugged my arm, "Here we are, Wes, my friend! You and me, 3rd and 4th grade. Miss Jenkins is our teacher. You will love her! When she hugs you, she always has a flowery smell."

I already knew her from church. She was the barber's wife. She had shiny black hair pulled into a bun in the back. Since her husband had gray hair, I thought of them as sort of grandparent age.

Miss Jenkins was skinny as a fence rail and had wrinkles. I elbowed Burley as we walked to take a seat. "Look at her fingernails painted so red. Aren't they beautiful?" She was soft-spoken and was never cross with us about anything. As Burley had predicted, I loved her.

Each time when we came in from recess, we tore off a sheet of paper from the big roll on top of our bookcase. That paper was our canvas to draw and color on while Miss Jenkins read to us from a children's mystery book.

If we got sleepy, it was okay to put our head down for a minute and rest. One day Terry Roberts snored so loud the entire class erupted in laughter, waking him from his nap! Miss Jenkins laughed too and said, "It's alright, Terrance, go on back to resting."

From the book she was reading to us, I only remember one name: the hero kid's dog, Brick. He was a big red dog, with a long shiny coat. When I told Mama about the story, she said Brick was probably an Irish Setter. "They are pretty dogs, like a redheaded little girl you might see."

The book was in progress when I got there, and we finished it not long before school was out. The story ended with Brick dying. I tried to hide my tears but didn't need to worry since most of the class was crying.

Meanwhile, back to Mama's most excellent plan. She looked the piano over and began to see a plan coming together in her mind. She thought the piano might be good enough for us. If they hired her and the program went well, she could lobby for a newer model. She located a man who tuned pianos as a side job. He lived about 30 miles away. She got his price for coming to evaluate the piano, and the extra amount for tuning if it was functional enough to use. Mama priced music books and other supplies.

Mama wanted her ducks in a row. She was in this thing, tooth and toenail. With no teaching experience or much education, it could be an uphill battle. Quitting any higher education to marry Daddy put many things out of reach for her. But she was smart, had a beautiful voice and could play the piano. And there was a bit of experience with three years of teaching Sunday school before they got married. The hope was this might be enough to get them to give her a chance.

Her idea was the older kids could do art and choir both. At first, the younger kids could start with just art and singing for fun. See how that would go. These classes would be one hour twice a week.

Over coffee, Mama told Miss Allie about her plan. She said, "Miss Allie has a finger on the pulse of the community."

"Betty, this music thing has been a burr under Miss Mac's saddle for a while. She will be inviting you and Duke to dinner soon, as she does every new family and newlywed couple. That may be the right time for you to let her know your thoughts. But if there is no opportunity to speak to her, you can have her for coffee and a chat later."

"I appreciate your input, Alice. I'm feeling more confident as time goes on that I am supposed to do something for our school in regard to music, and I guess, art."

Daddy told me about this plan. "Mama said to Allie, it was you who clued me about Miss Mac's way of charming Mr. Mac. She is sort of the power behind the throne. If she likes something, she has a lot of pull with Mr. Mac for getting things approved."

"Of course, Allie agreed. Said something like it is the way the wind blows, and more is done in a short amount of time with the scent of perfume, than a hundred rooms full of cigar smoke and the bad smell!"

"What does that mean, Daddy?"

"Well, it means that men get together and sometimes take a long time to decide anything and may fuss with each other. But good women know how to treat men and that makes the men want to do things for them. The men don't get along so well with each other, but the smart ones love to get along with and please the little lady. You see?"

I did not see. But I took note of the one thing I did get: "Please the Little Lady." And I remember when I accidently held Mary Lee's doll when it was important to do so. Later on, Daddy told me more secrets about this. All very helpful.

Mama decided to wait for the dinner invitation before she said anything else to anybody about her plan for music at school.

School had been in session for two weeks when Mrs. Mac called to invite us. Their house was set a little ways apart from the rest of us. It had outbuildings around it, looked like a complex of sorts. I saw tennis courts, horses, dogs and chickens. Their kids had friends over often. There was an end-of-school party every year that the whole school attended.

The house loomed large on the landscape as visitors approached. It was a small castle! That evening we learned the McCleary's had six children filling the spaces in that enormous house: two girls, two boys, and a set of twins who were a boy and a girl. We had heard the McCleary's were unable to have children, so each of these kids were adopted as babies.

I could see right away it was a fun, noisy household. The kids were close. Older ones looked out for the younger. They seemed happy. There was much laughter and unbridled talking.

I thought of myself and Mary Lee in homes where we were the only kid. How different it must be to have so many siblings. It must be a continual exciting adventure with so much going on. I didn't want to feel envious, but I knew I was missing something by being an only child. I didn't give it much thought until something like having dinner with the McCleary family came along.

Mr. McCleary mentioned that every business on the ranch was owned by the ranch. "The people who manage the stores work for the ranch just like you do, Duke. The stores are operated on a for-profit basis. Then the profits go into the town's bank account for paying salaries, the usual repairs and such that a town needs."

Daddy asked, "What about a governing body. Is there a mayor and town counsel?"

"There is a duly elected mayor and four town council members. Every monthly council meeting is open to anyone who wants to attend. There is no police force because there has never been a need for one. The town council also serves as a court to settle disputes between neighbors, which are not that many."

Mrs. Mac smiled, "Mac and I had an ideal town in mind, but it is even above and beyond what we had hoped for. We are living our dream, to be sure!"

Mr. Mac laughed. "Oh, Mackie, you do go on! But folks, it is true. We have succeeded very well here, and I have some things on the back burners for later on, too." It seems "Mackie" is his nickname for Miss Mac, but no one else calls her that.

I was interested in the workings of the town, and how the ranch was run. I had never heard of some of what they talked about that night. But it stuck with me.

I was one of those kids who paid attention to the adult conversations around me.

Within days, Mama invited Miss Mac for coffee to discuss her plan, and by sundown it was a done deal! Mama was authorized to implement her art and music program. The school board would finalize it and set her salary when they met.

Mama thought she would start next year, but Miss Mac told her, "Oh no, Sweetie, you start a week from today!"

It wasn't long before we all felt secure and happy at Mesquite Creek Ranch. Mama said more than once, "It was a God thing that we came here."

The second Saturday after school started, Burley came to our house on a mission. He knocked and I went to the door. "Hey, Wes Man, I want to check out your chicken pen and coop. You need to make sure it will hold in your chickens."

"I have kinda been waiting for my Daddy, Burles. But he is so busy learning about the ranch and all. Maybe it's something you and me could manage together. I don't know much, but I'm a quick learner!"

"Exactly, my plan. Exactly!" He smiled---the happiest guy I ever met.

We went out back, and there was a wheelbarrow with a wire cage holding seven hens and a rooster. I could hardly believe my eyes.

"These hens were donated by your friendly neighbors to help you become a chicken farmer! This red one and that black are a year old. They hatched in my flock. Miss Allie donated the speckled one, two years old, a good layer. The two white ones are five years old, laying hit and miss. They came from Miss Bessie Travis. Those two brown speckled ones came from Ozzie's dad. They are about a year old and laying really well. And that handsome fellow there is a purebred Mesquite Creek Ranch Chicken---meaning its actual family tree is not known to anyone."

Burley was beaming, and I was so excited I could hardly get my breath.

"Burley, this is so great!" He had a grocery bag about half full of laying feed, a hammer, and a box of nails. There were two old enamel pans that had seen better days. We inspected the fence on all sides. It was in excellent condition. Inside the coop, we cleaned out the next boxes. Burley unloaded the wheelbarrow then went home and brought back a load of hay for using in the nests and coop floor. There were eight nests built along one wall of the coop, and roosts on the back wall.

"What about the weeds in the yard, Burley. Should we mow or chop them with the hoe?"

"Don't worry none--those will disappear in a few days once the chickens get in there."

We put out the two enamel pans, one with feed--the other with water.

"Clean water and at will feeding is a must. The best way is to get an automatic water thing that fills up when they drink. That way they have clean water all the time. Feed buckets work about the same. They have a tray at the bottom. When the chickens eat, more pellets come out into the tray."

"I had no idea, Burley. My Daddy has never kept chickens either, so this advice is great. I will tell him we need to get these handy feed and water gizmos and save ourselves some headache there."

Then, one by one, Burley took a chicken out, handed it to me, and I slipped it in the gate close to the ground. As soon as I let go, they ran off.

"Be sure you hold the wings tight to her sides, but if she gets them free and starts flapping, don't let go or she will run off, and a dog might get her before we do."

Twice I didn't get a grip, and they flapped like crazy. "Hold on, Wes, get her in the gate!"

Some others I got ahold of squawked their displeasure of the whole thing. They all hit the ground running. One walked off cackling like she was the town fire alarm. It took about 10 minutes for her to shut up. But we got them all into the pen.

The rooster didn't fight at all. He mostly clucked rapidly as if he might be insulted. I set him down. He shook his feathers and walked off slowly. Then he stood there like he was getting his bearings. The ladies had already run into the weeds and were pecking away. Then he seemed to realize he was the only guy around. There were no competitors. He talked to the ladies and showed them tidbits or a bug, he found on the ground.

Burley was happy with my progress. "My goodness alive, Wesley, you have took to this chicken keeping like a duck to water. I'm proud of you!"

"I couldn't have done it without you, my Burley-man!"

Chapter 11

My rooster was a beautiful bird. He was decked out with a black feathered head sporting a red comb, black, brown-greenish and golden colors on this body. His tail was mostly iridescent black with the feathers arching nicely.

As I expressed my admiration of him, Burley chuckled. "Hmm! When it comes to him, you're a lifesaver. Daddy had him in our chicken yard in line for Sunday dinner!"

"Well, I guess that means he's lucky. I was thinking of calling him Handsome. But, Lucky, it is!"

"I don't know about a duck to water, but I know I'm worn out with just that little bit we did."

"You may have to herd them into the coop at dusk. But once they sleep and wake up there, it will be like home for them."

"How do I herd chickens? I never thought of such a thing."

"Aw, there's nuthin' to it. Just get a weed or stick or something like that to wave them on with. Just shoo them slowly. If your Daddy or Mama helps you, two is better than one. They will go in fairly easy. Just don't crowd them."

That first day, I went back and forth checking on my flock. Mama did, too. I found an egg on the ground, which was quite exciting. Burley was my chicken advisor. I consulted him almost daily for weeks.

That night, Daddy and I shooed them toward the coop. They went in, milled around looking up at the roosts. Lucky jumped up first. He clucked and stomped his feet on the wooden roost rail, going back and forth talking to the ladies. The ladies began one by one to get up there with him.

The next day, when I woke up, the first sound I heard was Lucky crowing. I dressed quickly and went out to open the coop. All were present and accounted for.

Daddy and I went to town after breakfast. We bought laying feed and a metal feeder. We got a water bowl with a floating thing that made it refill when they drank. And its hose hooked up to the spigot that was already there.

In the afternoon as the sun was dipping low, I went out with a small bowl Mama gave me to see if we had eggs. In the coop, there was one on the floor still clean enough to use, and three others in the nests. I was so happy and excited. Another great day at the ranch! And, I was in the chicken business. Wes Redmond The Chicken Farmer. Not exactly The King Ranch, but I was plenty proud!

My first semester of school (3rd grade) I started out like my chickens—in a strange place and needing to adapt! I made mostly A's. The last day of the semester came and went. We were all ready for summer! But there was a big surprise coming up for me.

The livestock tanks ("dirt tanks") were crucial to farm and ranch survival. Big machinery built these round earth structures with high sides and a deep bowl in the middle. The center was packed with hard clay to hold the water. This was the water source for people, animals, and plowed fields. Electric pumps sunk deep in the ground brought the water up.

The dirt tank was also where most farm and ranch kids learned to swim. When Mama told me there were swimming lessons at a ranch nearby, it sounded like fun.

Mama drove the pickup into a mowed field and parked with the other vehicles. There were parents and kids everywhere--mostly kids around my age and younger.

Daddy had explained why I had to take swimming lessons. "The creek swimming hole is safe, but only for those who know how to swim. If you don't learn to swim, you won't be getting into the creek."

"I think I'm old enough now that I can learn, Daddy. I don't want to be the only kid who can't swim!"

"That's the spirit, Son! You are just the right age-- almost nine years old. You are ready Freddie for summer fun."

I remember vividly that cool early summer morning. I was excited about this new adventure--learning to swim.

We walked up the side of the packed earth hill, stood on the wide rim and looked across at what seemed like a lake to me. It was a very large expanse of water. Suddenly, I was full-on terrified.

There was a wooden platform floating on several 55-gallon drums in the middle of the lake. In order to pass the swimming test, I had to swim out to the platform and swim back. We could rest at the platform if we needed to. My problem was, even after I learned to swim, I could not swim that far. (My fear made me hyperventilate.)

The adults who were in the water with us helped us to learn to kick our feet and use our arms in the water, while their hand underneath us held us up. Every time the woman teaching me would let her hand down, I would panic and start to sink. One by one, the other kids swam and made it out to the platform and back. Even kids two years younger than me could do it.

We went back day after day. Finally, I was swimming well enough, but I could not make it to the platform. They had to rescue me and take me back to where I could touch bottom. It was the last day of lessons. I was with the younger kids who were not going to get a certificate.

Chapter 12

The lady who was working with me, Nanette, had an idea for how I could do this.

"Wes, you can swim, but you get out of breath and need to take a rest. I'm gonna show you how to float on your back. So, when you know you need to get your breath, you can roll on your back, relax, and rest until you can breathe again. I will be right there with you treading water in case anything goes wrong."

"Thank you for taking time with me, Miss Nanette. I'm going to give it all I got this time. I want my certificate!"

Floating was easy. Nanette let me practice.

"Are you ready, Wes?" "Yes, Ma'am I am!"

I swam about halfway to the platform, then rolled onto my back. Nanette came over to me, but she didn't help me. She let me see her there. If she helped me, I wouldn't get my certificate.

I floated for a long time until I was no longer gasping for air. Then, I swam to the platform where I rested again for a short time. I was feeling confident. I turned to swim back, but didn't get far before I felt the fatigue and panic set in. I had to float.

When I started swimming again, I saw I was still a long way from the bank. But this time, I was not going to stop! I was NOT going to panic! I kept swimming.

I could hear everybody on the bank shouting. I had my friends and the parents backing me up, cheering me on to keep going!

"Go Wes Go!" "You're gonna make it!" And I did!

Mama said how proud she was, and she told Daddy all about it when he came home that evening. He said, "Ain't you glad now that you did this, Wes? You should be very proud!"

I thought a minute. "No. I hope I never have to swim again in my whole life."

They both got a big laugh, and I was confident they had no idea how hard the swimming lessons were for me. Even though I got my certificate that did not remove the humiliation I felt, not to mention the FEAR.

The years went by and Adult Me finally got over the feeling of panic when I got around water deeper than a bathtub. I am still not "a swimmer" by any stretch of anybody's imagination. But I am able to swim in water over my head without needing help.

I waded in the Pacific Ocean to get my feet wet and be able to say I did it. I stayed close to the shoreline. (Monsters of the deep, rip tide and all that.) I watched over the little ones who wanted to dig in the sand. My wife was the one who swam like the fishes and watched over our bravest land-locked older kids.

More than once at the Nueces River here in Texas, I got a running start, swung on the rope tied to a Mesquite tree limb and let go as I dropped into the deep river water. Then without too much fear, I managed to get back to the bank, and do it again! It was kind of fun and high adventure for a "chicken" like me.

Mainly, I wanted to be brave for my children. I didn't want them to discover the terror behind my eyes as I encouraged them to give it a try. I even swung out with my two little girls holding on to me their first time.

I wanted them to see Daddy as a hero, not a wimp!

Whether it was dropping into deep water from a rope, riding horses or even more terrifying--a Spelling Bee or book report, I mostly supported my kids in what they wanted to try, and understood their angst if they wanted to quit.

It seems to me that some of our experiences in childhood may leave indelible marks on our memory. They may be a part of our psyche forever.

I would not force children to do something like that if they didn't want to. And even though I wanted to learn to swim, and did, I still have a fear of the water.

I also was not a kid who would take a dare. I would face humiliation and hazing from others rather than push myself to do something stupid or scary to me. I knew my limits.

I was so glad Burley was my friend. He was always brave but patient with those who were not! Always there, ready to assist timid, nerdy kids to look for a bit more courage.

If he had been with me at the dirt tank, I likely would have made it to the platform and back a lot sooner than I did. My instructor Nanette was knowledgeable, patient and kind, but she was not Burley!

A few days later, Burley and I were in his room working on putting together a model airplane. Burley's grandmother had sent it to him. Neither of us had ever done a model. My mind wasn't in it. I was thinking about other things. Mulling over something I had wondered about for a while.

"Burley, why doesn't Mary Lee go to school?"

"You know that she's kinda slow, don't you, Wes?"

I did know, and I was already praying that Mary Lee could be healed by the Lord or the doctors find a way for her to learn. I had a feeling there was something locked in her head, that needed to be unlocked.

I answered Burley's question. "Yeah. Mama told me she would grow up to be mentally only about twelve years old and no more. But did they ever try to get a special teacher for her or looked for a school where people like her could get help with learning. Did they do more than just believe the doctors and not try to help her?"

"Honestly, Wes, I don't know. She was taken to doctors and told the 12 years old part. Miss Baker tries to help her and wants her to be able to go to school. But she doesn't want the other kids to make fun of her. It was when she was little and had trouble back then. I don't know if they have looked for other help since then."

"Well, I know she can learn things. I sang her a silly song, I learned at my last school. I sang it, and she clapped her hands and laughed, saying, "Sing it again!"

So, I sang it again, and she sang most of it with me. Now she requests it all the time. And she sings the harmony!"

"What song did you sing?"

I laughed and sang;

> *Ol' Dan Tucker was a mighty man,*
> *Washed his face in the fryin' pan.*

> *He combed his hair with a wagon wheel,*
> *Died with a toothache in his heel.*

> *Get out the way ol' Dan Tucker,*
> *You're too late to stay for supper.*

> *Supper's over, breakfast cookin',*
> *Ol' Dan Tucker standing lookin'.*

Burley slapped his knee and hee-hawed!

He smiled, "You know, Wes, you have a limp in your leg, and that makes you understand Mary Lee's limp in her head. And, this part the Lord showed me: you and her have a strong connection, more than my connection with her. We are both her brothers, but you are the favorite."

At this point, he grinned broadly, adding, "You seem to have a strong bond with little Mary Lee."

"She is the first friend I met when I got to the ranch, Burley. I will never stop being her friend. I am going to fight for her. I want you to help me, too. She won't stand a chance to get better as long as the grown-ups keep finding reasons why she can't even try!"

After that, I began working with her, trying to teach her to read. She was making progress. She was learning. She had come out of her shyness quite a bit, too. Once away from her hearing me, I told Miss Irene it would be good to let her start in first grade.

"That would be good, Wes, except she is so much older and bigger than little first graders. I don't want them or her to feel odd in class. She would be a misfit there."

"Okay, Miss Irene. I can understand that. But there has to be some kind of a plan to help Mary Lee. I believe she should be given a chance."

"Well, that would be the ideal, Wes. And you're a sweet young man to care so much."

I was disappointed because I knew that she could learn and improve. And, even her Mama didn't believe it.

Of course, as usual, Burley was all for it, and he began to help me teach her little things no one ever explained to her. Like playing checkers. She caught on to that in nothing flat and loved to play. I helped her read some of my comic books. The sentences were short and so were the words. She remembered words with three or four letters, and how to print them. She can write her name: Mary Lee Baker. She made sentences: I am here. Wes is nice. I like him. I was doing the "See Dick run. Go Jane go" thing with her.

Mama got involved. She began teaching Mary Lee a bit of meal preparation. She wanted to help around the kitchen. Her Mama did everything for her but spoon feeding! In reality, Miss Irene was holding her back in many ways.

Mary Lee learned how to make a sandwich, toast in the toaster, and other simple things. She knew the difference between a table knife and the sharp ones that would cut her. I didn't use the sharp knives either, that made it easier for her to feel like that was normal. She was okay with leaving the sharp ones alone.

She wasn't "cooking" as such, but she became a whiz at peanut butter and jelly sandwiches and roast beef sandwiches with mustard. She could wash lettuce, set the table, and do other meal prep things, like snapping green beans from the garden.

She shocked her Mama one day as she wrestled with escaped jelly on their kitchen counter. She was smearing it with the dishcloth.

"What in the world are you tryin' to do, Sweetie?"

"I'm fixing me a sandwich like Wesley's Mama taught me, but this time the jelly got away and just went wild!" She had jelly on her clothes and hands.

That's when Miss Irene found out we were letting her do things at our house. She wasn't upset with us at all. She told Mama she could see that she wasn't letting the girl do even what she could!

There were other mishaps, of course, but Miss Irene didn't get angry with her for messing up or with us for butting in. She saw right away there was hidden potential, and Mary Lee certainly had the will to learn.

"I am in need of learning myself. I have been holding her back." Mama said Miss Irene cried about it.

Burley and I talked to Brother Harvey, and he was all over this plan for getting help for Mary Lee. He was eager to find out what could be done to help this along.

He said, "Well, boys, I certainly agree with Irene that first grade is not the place for her. But I think she might do well with some special one-on-one teaching and being in class with kids her age."

Burley exclaimed, "She will be safe in class with Wes and Miss Jenkins will be just the one to help her get going. Nobody will make fun of her." Of that fact, I was very sure. The Power of The Burley One is love!

So, Brother Harvey talked with the McCleary's and Miss Jenkins. They brainstormed about what they might do. How could she be taught at her grade level and still be in her age group. And how could we get Mary Lee's parents on board.

Brother Harvey thought Burley and I should ask Mary Lee what she thought about going to school with us now that she was older. We were sort of testing the waters. We wanted to have Mary Lee's okay before we talked with her parents.

We brought it up to her kind of casual like. I explained to her that Miss Jenkins would work with her like I had. And she might learn faster because Miss Jenkins was a real teacher. Mary Lee was excited and ready to go.

She told her parents before we had the chance.

Miss Irene said Mary Lee was very matter of fact, "You should talk to Burley and Wes about me going to school. I want to go!"

Chapter 13

[September 1952, 4th grade, 9 years old]

The parents of 3rd and 4th graders got a notice the week before school started. Mrs. Jenkins wanted to gather with them at school. She discussed the whole thing concerning Mary Lee. Some already knew about this from the tom-toms around the ranch.

True to the heart of Mesquite Creek Ranch "code" these moms and dads were glad to be of help, so this little girl has a chance to work toward discovering her potential. Brother Harvey attended the meeting and emphasized the importance of the other kids not making fun of Mary Lee and accepting her as one of them.

One of the dads spoke up saying. "I think these kids will accept Mary Lee. They've known her all their lives. But parents can make sure by speaking to them about it and teaching them to help by encouraging her."

Burley asked Miss Jenkins if he could speak to the parents. He stood before a room full of adults and said, "Miss Irene picked me as the person to watch out for Mary Lee when she mingles with us kids. If you explain to your kids--about me looking out for Mary Lee and that she needs to be included as much as we can, there will be no problems with her among the classmates. I am sure."

This was Burley's way of letting all the kids know that they will NOT say or do anything to make fun of Mary Lee Baker. And, of course, they didn't.

Once we got the ball rolling, Burley and I together were better able to get Mary Lee to join in. She would hang around with other girls, but still preferred Burley and me. But, in the weeks before school started, all three of us were telling the kids she would be coming to school with us. The girls squeaked and squealed, jumping up and down. She has her own cheering section!

When we talked to her parents, her Daddy said they needed to at least try the plan with her being in the fourth grade with me. There was nothing to lose as things stood at the moment with her progress. Miss Irene was a bit more over-protective, but she agreed. I think she felt guilty for not helping Mary Lee more. Mama told her gently, "Mary Lee needs special teaching with expertise that we are not trained to do, Irene."

Things fell in place quickly for The Continuing Education of Mary Lee Baker.

The great rush for school clothes and odds and ends, which Mary Lee had never done, was fun for her. We made one more trip into Roca for Burley to find a pair of boots big enough for him. Miss Whit drove us. Mary Lee went, too. Burley found the right fit and even the color he wanted. Then we went to the coffee shop diner for lunch.

When we were eating, Mary Lee said, "I can hardly wait for school. I know that you boys did this for me. Mama told me you did. If I turn out to be smart, it is because the two of you believed that I could. If it turns out another way, it's okay, because I will still love you and we can be friends like always!"

Burley and I stopped chewing and looked at each other. I had the highest hope I ever had for anything in my life before or since that day! I remember her then like it was yesterday.

Miss Whit dabbed her eyes with her napkin.

That first day of school was hectic. Everybody was excited. All of us knew Mary Lee was joining us without the benefit of 1st through 3rd grade. She was behind in every way there was! But true to the code of our village, every kid from 4th grade up wanted to make her feel like she was part of us and help her to succeed at being a third/fourth grader.

I would whisper to her and even sit beside her in her desk chair, trying to help her. Miss Jenkins didn't scold me for breaking that rule. She no doubt knew this helped Mary Lee psychologically as much as it did academically. We did better when we got home, and I could help her at one kitchen table or the other without distractions.

But several weeks into the semester, Miss Jenkins asked me to stay after the bell. In our meeting, Miss Jenkins had to be blunt.

"You cannot be her teacher all the time, Wes. You need to be learning things yourself. Your homework is not up to speed with last year. I think you're spending too much of your homework time teaching Mary Lee."

Miss Jenkins was right. Mrs. Baker should help her at home. I actually think it was better for her, too. And, she did better in class without me hovering. She gained confidence at home and brought it with her to school.

That first week of school on Friday, Miss Jenkins had an announcement. "After mid-term exams, we will have our Christmas party the day school lets out. I want each of you to give a gift of your talent to the class. It can be a few of you getting together to do a skit, telling a funny joke, a solo on a musical instrument, singing, reciting or reading a poem, whatever you can think of. Does anyone have an idea already?"

Several hands shot up. Miss Jenkins was thrilled "Good, now that's a start!"

On the way home from school, Burley gave me a shoulder bump. "Okay, Wes, you and Mary Lee are going to do Ol' Dan Tucker!" Mary Lee giggled. "Yes, we are!!"

Now, I had a new thing to add to my anxiety folder: Stage Fright. It follows me into my adult years. I am more of an introvert, in spite of how much of a talker I am. I never quite got over standing to speak before an audience, but I do it when I have to.

So, I sweated it out until time for our duet! But when our big moment came, we sang the verse twice, and Mary Lee had a blast. Her harmony was perfect. Our friends cheered us on. It was great. I would have done it again and again just to see how happy she was.

Burley didn't tell me he would be singing, too. He had asked Miss Jenkins if he could go last. He stood, explaining that this song was about remembering long gone mothers, and honoring the ones we still have with us. It was a lullaby sung to babies by Irish American immigrants when America was a newborn nation—a baby herself.

Then he sang in a most beautiful voice, and with an Irish accent, a song I had never heard: *An Irish Lullaby.*

Over in Kilarney, Many years ago.
Me Mether sang this song to me,
In tones so sweet and low.

'Twas a simple little ditty, in her fine ol' Irish way,
But I'd give the world to hear her sing
that song to me today.

Toor-a-lur-a-lur-a, toor-a-lur-a-ly,
toor-a-lura-lura. . . hush now don't you cry.
Toor-a-lur-a-lur-a, toor-a-lur-a-ly,
toor-a-lura-lura . . . It's an Irish lullaby.

This is something else I remember vividly. When the lullaby ended, on a sweet and very high note sustained with all his breath, there was utter silence for several seconds as several classmates, Miss Jenkins, Mary Lee, me, and Burley himself had tears flowing over their cheeks. Then, as much thunderous applause as 18 or so kids could make, and whistles so loud and piercing others in school wanted to know what happened at our party they didn't get at theirs! Burles was a hero, and sadly may have had the least loving mother of us all!

That weekend, it was a good fall day, not hot or cold. We had a great time--all the kids were out in full force. I ate lunch with Mary Lee and Burley. His Mama made soup. She served it up and disappeared. Mary Lee said

106

we should wash our bowls and put the soup in the fridge. She used the dish cloth to wipe up the cornbread crumbs on the table.

I walked Mary Lee home and went on to my house. I saw Miss Allie was there. She had been crying--either for a long time or real hard. Maybe it was both. She looked heartbroken.

She got up to leave, but Mama said, "No, Sweetie, keep your seat." She steered me back to the door and out on the porch.

"Were you at Burley's, Wes?"

I nodded. "Yes, ma'am. And I was at Mary Lee's too, earlier."

"Then where did you eat lunch?"

"At Burley's. Miss Whit made a great soup and cornbread."

"Okay. Go on over to the Baker's and see if they can give you some supper. Miss Allie is fit to be tied right now, and I need to stick with her. With your Daddy off in Smithville looking for a new bull, he won't be home before dark. If I don't call you before bedtime, just spend the night with Burley."

This kind of a thing isn't common in our village, taking care of each other's kids on such short notice. But it isn't unheard of or strange. It's what we do here.

I walked over to Mary Lee's. She was glad to see me, like I hadn't just spent most of the day with her.

"I need to talk with your Mama. There's a problem at my house."

She was immediately on high alert. She looked horrified, she scrunched her dress with both hands, and she bent her knees up and down, making her Shirley Temple curls bounce like crazy. Then, with her leading the way, we went inside with her hollering, "Mama, oh, Mama, there's a problem over at Wesley's house!"

Miss Irene looked at me, but she was calm. I shook my head like "no." She was accustomed to Mary Lee's over the top response with anything unusual. "Now, calm down, Sweetheart, let Wesley tell us."

"Miss Allie is the one with the problem. She has been with Mama for some time, I think, and her eyes are red and swollen. That's all I know; except I am being farmed out to you folks for supper! Will that work for you, Miss Irene?" I had a nervous little laugh, hoping it didn't seem stupid under the circumstances.

Miss Irene chuckled. "Now then, Wes, the problem of making sure you get supper is easy as pie for a gal like me. But the problem with your Mama and Miss Allie is likely something we have faced before--a job for the Lord, I think. Meanwhile, you two kids get you a game of checkers going, while I see about supper."

We went on out to the porch. I heard Miss Irene talking on the phone to Mama. The conversation was brief, so I figured Mama must have things more or less under control.

Mr. T.J. drove up not long after we had played our second game of checkers. He spoke to us as he stepped up on the porch, and patted Mercy.

"How you kids doing'? You got any idea what's for supper tonight?" Neither of us said anything about Miss Allie.

"Sorry Daddy, we don't know what Mama's making tonight."

"You staying over, Wes."

"Yes, Sir, I am. Sort of invited myself."

He grinned. "Glad to have you, Son."

Soon we got called inside. "It's getting cool out here. You two come in." I don't even remember what we ate. I remember Mr. T.J. praying for Miss Allie.

After saying "amen" as he was buttering his bread, Mr. T.J. commented, "So, same ol' thing, with Alice, is it?"

Miss Irene nodded and said, "Yup. Same thing."

Mama never called me, so when it got going for bedtime, I went on over to Burley's. I looked back at our house, saw the porch light was on, but the house was dark. Daddy's truck wasn't there. My thought was that they went to Brother Harvey.

I was plenty curious to know what was going on with poor Miss Allie. But kids had to be careful. Sometimes, more was learned by listening quietly than asking questions.

I got to Burley's and was welcome to stay the night. We made a bed on his bedroom floor with quilts. Miss Whit called it a "Baptist Pallet." We were spreading the quilts, as I told the two of them about what took place at my house. I could tell Miss Whit knew. She looked at Burley kind of funny but didn't say anything. "Mama, you might as well tell him, everybody on the ranch over the age of six knows what's wrong with Miss Allie."

Chapter 14

Burley's Mama said, "I guess. Okay. Wes, when Miss Allie was a young wife, she wanted children. The doctors said she has some problem called in-der-me-o-sus or something like that, and it made her where it would take a miracle for her to ever have a baby. It also is a hurtful condition in the body, making her sick with pain at times. The doc said they needed to do surgery to get it out. But it meant she would never give birth. She prayed for a miracle, but it never came."

"She was in so much pain with it she finally gave in. They took out the baby carriage. She tries to face being childless. She does okay for long stretches by helping other people and staying busy. At times she's peaceful and happy for a year or so. But sooner or later, it hits her. She goes into a nosedive down the rabbit hole."

I remembered that thing I saw in her eyes when we were in the Soda Shop that first day we got to the ranch. This was it. It was a horrible sorrow.

"She trusts your Mama, Wes. Your Mama went for a time, thinking she would never have another baby after you. It's a tragedy, is what it is, when a lady is longing for babies so bad like that. But Allie--she's tougher than these storms that come over her. She has faith in her God. I don't know why, but she does. And it seems to help her."

With that, Miss Whit looked at me, then at Burley. She sighed, and turned to leave the room saying, "Goodnight, boys. You pray for her, you hear?"

I turned toward Burley. I knew the "why have faith in God" comment bothered him. We didn't speak for a couple of minutes. Then, he said, "We should pray for her." I said, "We should pray for your Mama, too." He nodded. He stared at me as a single tear slid down his cheek. I said, "You pray for Miss Allie and I'll pray for your Mama. Okay?"

He nodded, wiped his eyes, and slipped off the bed on to his knees. I moved over from my pallet to kneel beside him.

"Dear Father in heaven, it's me, Burley. Poor Miss Allie almost loses her mind when these spells come over her. It seems like a devilish attack. We pray for your mercy over her, and for wisdom for Miss Betty and Mr. Duke and Mr. Tim and whoever else is with her right now. Let her know the peace that passes understanding. Amen."

I continued our prayers, "Now, Lord, for Miss Whit, Burley's Mama, who is lost as Hogan's goat! I, Wesley, pray for her now. You see her surrounded at this ranch and in her own house, by people who believe in You, and love her. She cannot escape Your Spirit that lives all around us. A lot of prayers go up for her. One day, her heart will be open and be healed. She will come to The Cross and be blessed. Make it so, Lord, because we ask these favors in the Name above all names, Jesus. Amen."

Burley was crying softly. I felt the urge to cry myself. But instead, I said . . .

"And, Lord, please touch Burley. Put joy in his heart and make him strong in Your Spirit. Hear our prayers and see our sadness for the people we care about. Let us give our problems and the problems of others to You, so we have a peaceful sleep. Amen."

We didn't go to sleep right away. We talked. Burley with concerns for his Mama, me with concerns for Mary Lee, and both of us trusting the Lord and believing that our prayers for Miss Allie were heard.

Burley thought, "My Daddy loves my Mama in spite of the way she doesn't believe. I don't know how he keeps on going year after year. But I will remember this and if my Godly wife I marry makes me want to run away from her, I will remind myself of what it means for a man to really LOVE his wife."

I was talking about my feelings for Mary Lee. I said, "I am so happy to have found her, and that she is getting to go to school. I really want her to succeed at learning and be smart like other people. She wants that real bad."

I heard a snore. I turned over and hugged Mercy. I was glad she was always welcome at Burley's house and the Baker's too.

I whispered prayers for my parents. And thanked God for all that they mean to me. I felt like I had the best parents in the world. There was great peace in our home most all the time. I always knew when they had a tiff. I never heard anything, but I could see it on their faces and the sort of disgusted, stiff way they kissed goodbye.

Burley and I both slept soundly and woke up refreshed. I thanked them for putting me up for the night and went home to see about my folks.

Mama filled me in on Miss Allie. It was mostly like Miss Whit had said. Miss Allie had a psychiatrist at one time, but all he wanted to do was give her medicine that turned her into another person that wasn't her!

"Allie told me it isn't anything that triggers the spells of this dark depression. She is just suddenly gripped by it. She loves being around children. But there are times of heart aching that just won't stop."

I was distressed, thinking about us not getting another baby and Miss Allie not having one at all. "Couldn't they adopt a baby? Like the McCleary's did."

Mama looked so sad as she kept going with telling me the facts. "That would be one solution except the process of being investigated by the State adoption people would turn up her medical records with mental problems, and they would never let her have a child. It seems like Allie and Tim just have no options at this point."

"Brother Harvey got her somewhat calm. The cowboys located Tim. He was at the Whistle, shooting some pool. But when he walked in the door, Allie ran to his arms, saying it was all gonna be alright---over and over. He knew exactly what was wrong."

I puzzled over it all. Her surgery that had taken away all hope. The McCleary's adopted six kids and she can't snag even one! What is that? I recalled things Mama said when we were talking about God. He knows the beginning to the end and all the in-between.

The days were flying by. Mary Lee was doing well in school, loving every bit of it. She was having the time of her life.

Mama begin to lose vim and vigor. She was happy as could be, but she felt tired all the time. Daddy was cheery about it. "You're just worn out from all the hassle of moving and working with the music program at school. You just need to catch up on your rest."

"I could be anemic. Maybe I need to eat more beef. I don't know."

I could tell Mama was not okay. It was more than just tired from moving here. I didn't know what anemic was. But I knew Mama was not herself.

Then, I began to get caught up with preparations for school. Mama wasn't talking very much about being so tired. I got caught up with my school doings. And, like the kid I was, I forgot all about it. When we went to shop for my school clothes, we went on Saturday. Daddy went with us. I didn't notice that was unusual.

Out of the blue one morning at breakfast, Mama announced, "I'm going to the doctor in Roca today to see why I'm so tired. Wes, when school is out, if we are not home, you go on over to the Baker's. Okay?"

"Sure, Mama. I will." Again, I missed that it was "I" going to the doctor, but "we" coming home. A slip of the lip I missed. Daddy went to the doctor with her. Not a good sign, if I had noticed.

That afternoon, when I got home, Daddy's truck was there. I wondered why, having forgotten the doc visit. I heard them talking quietly in their room. I went into my room, shut the door, and 1 laid across my bed with Mercy. We went sound asleep.

When I woke, I heard Mama's voice in the living room. I opened my door. Daddy said, "Wes, come on in here. Mama and I need to talk with you."

Fear gripped me, instantly. I remembered the anemic thing, the doc visit, Daddy home so early. My heart started to pound. Something was terribly wrong with Mama.

I'm sure I was white as a sheet when I walked in. They were sitting on the couch. Mama sat forward quickly. "Oh, no, Wes, it isn't anything bad!" She held out her arms.

I went over to them, and they both hugged me. They sat me on the coffee table in front of them, Mama still holding my hands. "Remember that time before we moved here when my back went out and I had to stay overnight in the hospital?"

"We thought it was best not to tell you what really happened then. I was carrying a baby -- didn't even know I was. It died. But now, guess what!"

"You got another baby?!"   "Yes! And this one is healthy!"

"Is it a girl or a boy?"   "Well, we won't know that until it's born."

"When will it be born?" "The doctor says it will be around Christmas."

"I want a sister!" "Well, me too, Honey, but every baby is a surprise!"

"Okay. And even if it's a brother, I will still love him to pieces!!"

I could not articulate well enough to say all I felt, so I cried.

I wailed, "I wanted us to have another baby my whole life."

Daddy laughed. "Me, too, Son!"

He took me up in his lap, gave me a squeeze. He kissed my forehead, then put his arm around Mama and squeezed us both tightly against himself.

"I can't stop thanking God. This is so wonderful! Oh, my little family!"

Daddy and Mama were staring into each other's eyes. He said, "You know, Betsy, this started the morning after we arrived at the ranch. Remember how rested we both felt, how relaxed and happy we were?"

Mama kind of blushed shyly. "Oh, listen to you go on! But I think you're right."

Much later, I had not forgotten that mysterious moment. I was thirteen years old, in "health" class. We were discussing the human gestation period. I realized then that counting backwards, December was nine months after we got to the ranch. And then there was a baby. Hmm?

We sat there for what seemed like a long time. So happy. The next morning Mama told me her plans.

"I'm gonna phone Miss Irene, Miss Alice, Miss Whit, and Miss Mac to come for coffee. I'll tell them the news. And you can tell Mary Lee and Burley on the way to school."

When I told them, Mary Lee immediately went into her own plans, chattering away. "Of course, I will be babysitting for your Mama whenever she needs me. I'm a very good babysitter. I will be a big help to her."

Burley was happy for us, too. "I'm so glad this has happened for you, Wes. You been waiting for this a long time."

When I came home from school, Mama fixed my after-school snack so I wouldn't faint before supper. She sat down with me at the table with a glass of tea. Then we traded stories about how excited our friends were about the baby.

"And, the ladies were all over-the-top happy for us, too. Even Miss Allie. She's over her spell of crying for now. They talked about what we need---a cradle, trundle bed, and on and on." Daddy laughed when Mama told him at supper. "I bet it sounded like a bunch of hens cackling for joy in here!"

After a few weeks, Mama was over being tired. She reasoned, "I'm over four months along now, the baby is fine, and I feel great. All is going well."

School whizzed by. In choir we were working hard on the Christmas music we would do. Mary Lee loved to sing. She was such a blessing to me.

Chapter 15

In early December Mama and I got out Christmas decorations, and Daddy cut us a small cedar tree from one of the back pastures. Mama was ready for the baby to come any time! Bobby Jo was managing the choir program for Christmas Eve. Mama was at home most of the time now, keeping off her feet to ease the swollen ankles.

Next project was midterm exams. Of course, Burley and I did well. Mary Lee was tested before she started school, so they had a baseline. She began above average for the beginning of First Grade. Mrs. Jenkins was surprised at Mary Lee's level and she knew it was the efforts of Burley and me who did that in a very short time. And her progress in one semester was very encouraging, she tested ready for Second Grade!

"The more she learns, the faster she will learn. I'll test the whole class this year. It's sort of standard, to know who might be lagging behind and needing help before going up to 5th grade."

Miss Irene spoke for us both. "I am so pleased she is learning and enjoying school the way she does. You are a great teacher. Are there materials we could get so I can work with her during the summer?"

"I will certainly give you some things for summer. And the best thing is to keep reading every day. It doesn't have to be hours, just whatever she wants to do. The library will have books to help with that. Get her books at second grade level and a few at third and see how she does. Throw in a Nancy Drew Mystery later on when she is older and ready for that level.

Miss Irene took the Three Musketeers to the library in Roca the next Saturday. Mary Lee loved the place! We all checked out books. She was excited to participate in the process and so proud of her library card.

The expected day for arrival of Mama's newest family member came a few days early. December 19th was our Christmas party in choir. Mama was there with us. She had elevated Burley to soloist in the choir. His Irish Lullaby was what prompted it.

Bobby Jo was our stand-in choir director. She was putting us through our paces with what we were doing with the church program for Christmas Eve. Mama was playing the piano. We sang with gusto, O Come All Ye Faithful. Burley would close the program with O Holy Night. Mama stopped in the middle of a verse. She walked around the piano and away from us. She didn't say anything. I got off the risers and went to her. Bobby Jo, Mary Lee, and Burley were right with me.

"Mama, are you all right?" She looked up at me. "You need to go to the office and phone Brother Harvey. The baby's coming."

The kids were getting down off the risers. I took charge. "Go back to class and let the teachers know the baby is coming."

Then I ran to the office, breaking the rule of not running in the halls. I blurted out the situation: "My Mama. . . the baby . . . Brother Harvey!!"

Miss Benton behind the desk responded, "You go back to your mother, I'll get Brother over here in a jiffy." I was only a little out of breath, so I ran all the way back. Mrs. Jenkins was fast-walking toward the music room.

I passed her up and got to where Mary Lee was walking around with Mama as B.J. timed the contractions. I marveled as the much excitable Mary Lee was calm as could be, and I was the basket case. Maybe it's a girl thing?

"Wes, I think there's not much time here before the baby comes. Not sure we can even make it into the hospital. Your Daddy . . ." Mama's voice trailed off.

Mrs. Jenkins was there. "Betty, let's start walking out. We can get in the car as soon as Brother Harvey gets here." Mama nodded.

We started down the hall with me on one side and Mrs. Jenkins on the other. Mary Lee was right with us. Of course, Burley was coming along, too.

The classroom doors were all open with teachers and kids crowded around to see what was going on with Mama. Some were standing inside, and others were lining up down the wall. They were all concerned, some not knowing what to think about all this.

Mrs. Jenkins was smiling at everyone, saying all was well, but I could see beads of sweat standing on her lip. She had a son herself, but I guess it's different when you are helping another person. I was so glad she was there with us.

We got out on the steps of the schoolhouse and Brother Harvey roared up. He helped Mama to the car and drove us to our house. Mama got into a big granny gown she had ready for this; she would lie down on the couch for a few minutes and then get up and walk around.

Miss Irene motioned to me. "Wes, you go on over to the bunkhouse and see if Cookie can come now. Tell him what's going on." It wasn't exactly close by. I took my shoes off to run faster. It wasn't much cold. Puffs of dust rose up as my feet slapped the powdered earth on the path. I burst through the door and ran to the kitchen. Cookie was stirring a pot of chili.

As fast as I could say it, I panted, "My Mama is having the baby. Mama wants to wait until Daddy gets home. Miss Irene told me to get you there fast."

Cookie smiled, wiping his hands on his big white apron. "Sit down, there, kid, take some deep breaths."

He turned the stove off, took off his apron, and wrote a note to the cowboys about cooking the chili another 20 minutes. He went into the larder and came back with what looked like a doctor's black bag.

He looked at me, grinning. He said with gusto, "Here we go, boy!" and grabbed my arm as we headed out the door running as fast as he could. When we got to the house, things were okay. Mama was walking around. She seemed for the most part, calm. But she wanted Daddy.

I was gasping for breath when we got there. I didn't know "come here" from "sic 'em" about all this. Nothing about the birthing of babies! Mama smiled, "It's all okay, Wes. Take a deep breath. Everything is going the way it should."

Cookie went over to the kitchen sink and started washing his hands up to his elbows with the Comet scrubbing powder Daddy used when he came in from work. He called me, "Look in my bag, Wes, and find a bottle of alcohol." I brought it to him.

He poured the alcohol over his hands and up to his elbows, saying, "Get me a clean dish towel and lay it over my hands," I did what he told me, including holding the towel by the edges to keep my hands off of it.

The ladies got Mama onto the bed. There was another clean sheet there. They covered her with it. They had already covered the bed with clean old quilts we used for picnics and such. Mama had this all laid out already.

Cookie and I came into the room. He told all of us to get out except Miss Irene. She closed the door behind us. We could hear them talking in mumbles. Mama groaned a little. In a short while, the door opened, and Cookie explained the situation.

"We need to go to the hospital right now! But she wants to wait a while on Duke." Brother Harvey stood up and went into the bedroom. Again, with the closed-door!! But he opened it almost immediately.

"We're going now."

Mama was up walking behind him and crying. The ladies got her to the car and into the back seat. She crawled in. I went in behind her and sat on the floor.

They tried to make me stay behind. "Nothing doing. I'm going with my Mama!"

Cookie, with his black bag, spoke with a calm voice. "Let's not argue, Wesley. I'll get in front, but if I need to, you will trade places with me. Okay?"

I nodded. And we took off. We got to the hospital in record time, Brother driving like a fireman. Mama was so brave. And Cookie rode in front all the way.

Just as the nurses got her on a stretcher and were ready to wheel her inside, a big pickup roared up with Mr. Tim driving. Daddy got out running to where Mama was.

The nurses stopped long enough for him to say, "It's all okay, Betsy." He leaned down and kissed her forehead.

She answered, "Yes, it is now that you're here!" Then they whisked her away.

Brother Harvey and Cookie brought Daddy up to speed, even told him how brave I was and how I helped. Then, Cookie smiled at me. "Well, Wes, it looks like we're partners now and practically obstetricians!"

I grinned back, "What is an obstetrician?"

"They are the docs who catch the babies when they're born."

He reached over and gave my arm a gentle sock.

After some time went by, Daddy looked at his watch. "It has been about fifteen minutes. We should know something soon now."

Right then, the doctor came in. "Mr. Redmond, your wife got here at the exact right time. Not much room to spare. She's a real trooper. You have a healthy baby girl, and she's a redhead. You can see them both in a few more minutes."

The doc turned and left quickly. I busted out bawling on the spot, and Daddy did, too. He hugged me. We sat down.

"Wes, I'm plumb weak-kneed. I don't know how these little women do that wonderful thing of birthing babies." I thought, yeah, I don't know how they do it either, knowing Daddy had to know more than I did!

Brother Harvey and Cookie were all into this. Cookie said, "I have to check on my patient and the littlest angel before I leave."

It wasn't long and they called for Daddy to come in. He took me with him. Mama didn't look too bad to me. Her face looked stressed, and her hair was messed up.

"Are you doing okay, Mama, did it hurt really bad for you."

She laughed and said one of Daddy's lines, "Well, it didn't tickle!! And that's for stinkin' sure!! But now, take it all the way around, I am blessed!"

We laughed. "I told you, Mama, it was a sister, and I was right!!"

She grinned, "Yes, you were!"

Chapter 16

The baby was tiny and her skin was reddish. I had never seen a newborn baby, only a couple that were a few weeks old. So, I had nothing to compare her to. But I didn't say anything except, "My baby sister. So special and precious to us. She is our baby, Mama."

I left out the part that she was really bordering on ugly. Her nose was flat, her eyes were too big for her face, and she had some serious wrinkles. Brother and Cookie came in to give kudos to Mama and coochie-coo to the latest Redmond specimen.

At this point, the hospital people wanted to fill out the birth certificate. I had thought about a name but was hesitant to say. Mama offered, "I had thought about Bella."

Daddy said, "Perfect! And, a middle name?"

I blurted out my name I thought of. "How 'bout Francine?" It sounded royal to me. I had been thinking about it for weeks.

Mama nodded, "Bella Francine it is, Wes." And, now we had the name for The Baby.

Daddy and I went home, leaving Mama and Bella to rest and practice nursing. I thought this meant giving her a bottle. Even as a child, I had more of a grasp on spiritual matters than a lot of adults. But when it came to Birds & Bees, I was hiding behind the door! I had seen dogs and cats, horses and cows, nursing their young! But . . . it was after Mama came home with Bella that I found out about breast feeding for humans.

That night, we tried to wind down. Mercy had been sleeping under the porch all day and wanted to chase her ball in the house. Daddy scrambled eggs and made toast for our supper. I threw the ball for Mercy. We sat a while not saying much. Daddy said, "I am feeling blessed." I said, "Yup. Me, too." Then we hit the sack.

"Our girls" as Daddy called them, stayed for two days at the hospital, then we brought them home. Bella was looking better. Her color was pinky white. She still didn't look too pretty, though. I wanted to help take care of her, but Mama said I had to wait until Bella was older.

People brought food for us and gifts for Bella--tiny little clothes and booties they had made. Mrs. Jenkins brought me a comic book, and she complimented me on being a good big brother--helping my Mama. Mary Lee came right away and was at our house every day during the holidays.

One couple who visited was Bobby Jo and Bubba Ledbetter. He was a Blue Ribbon Boy, 19 years old, and was raised on the ranch. He loved B.J. when she was in the 10th grade. She put the blue ribbon on that year, and he warned the other cowboys to keep their hands off of her. During her Senior year, they got engaged and married that summer. They lived with her folks until they got their own house in the married community.

At the time, they had been married over a year. Bobby Jo confided in Mama. "I want to have friends, not just rely on my Mama and her friends. We need some couple friends. But most everybody our age are all gone off to work or to college. And I feel like most of the married women here in the village think I'm a kid. I wish they could see that I'm doing my best to be a grown up! It isn't easy to be an instant adult."

Mama laughed with her, but this seemed to Mama like a plea for acceptance and friendship. Bubba and Daddy were having a beer while the girls talked. B.J. held the baby.

Mama was impressed with B.J.'s voice as she sang to Bella. And she did a fine job at our Christmas program in church. Mama was well enough to attend. Bella slept through it all!

Mama thanked her again for all she did for the choir program.

132

When Bubba and Bobby Jo were leaving, Mama told her, "You keep in touch, you hear? Come visit me soon."

Christmas was low key for us. Mama had gifts for Daddy and me. Daddy gave her a nice bottle of perfume. The Bakers had us to their house for Christmas dinner. Miss Irene even sent some leftovers home with us so we could get another meal out of it.

On Saturday, Mr. Tim called and talked to Daddy for a few minutes and then to Mama.

"How are you, Betty?" "I am doing really well, Tim. Getting a lot of rest. The baby is on a schedule of eat and sleep."

"That's great, right there! Now then, Allie is in the shower, so I want to make this short. She says she is okay with visiting. She wants to see the baby. She wanted to come over right away when you first got home. But I thought it might be a little soon for her. What do you think, Betty?"

"Well, Tim, none of us knows what will happen, not even Allie. She is in a tough fight with this thing. But sooner or later she is going to come over with or without you, so you might was well get it over with."

Miss Alice looked great. Had her makeup fixed. She had a fine time with the baby--holding her, burping her, and singing to her. She told Mama, "I'm so happy for you after what you have gone through. I have such joy for you, there is no way I could think about my own troubles now. I know I might have a meltdown again, but not while this baby is so close by, and I can come over and get a sniff of her any time I want."

We all laughed. It was obvious she was her old self again. She and Mama were best friends. I knew Mama was praying for Allie. Not asking God for anything, except Allie being happy with how things are. Sometimes that's just how life is. You aren't always happy because of the circumstances. At times, you're happy in spite of them.

And seeing others with joy in their blessings can become your joy, too.

Somewhere in all of this, the second semester of the school year went by in a flash.

There was a whirl wind around Bella. Our house was a hub. We also moved to a bigger house. I enjoyed the freedom of summer and hung out with Burley and Mary Lee a lot. I slept a lot too.

I got up early to take care of my chickens, but after lunch, I took a nap almost every day. We swam a lot too. That and the heat when biking or playing ball took the energy out of all of us. There was no big incidents or excitement to speak of. One thing that changed for us was B.J. and Bubba sort of getting adopted by us.

Chapter 17

[September 1953, 5th grade, 10 years old]

By the time I got to 5th grade, my limp was barely perceptible. Maybe as I grew my bad leg just caught up with the other one. Or, maybe the limp was psychosomatic--deep inside I was afraid to step hard on it. But either way, one day the limp was completely gone.

Before we were ready, summer was over. The calendar was into late August. Before we could figure it out, Labor Day was looming, and school would be in session again. The kids and their parents began the scramble to buy and sew clothes, and all that went with getting ready for a new school year back in that day.

Mary Lee and I were moving up. We were also back in class with Burley again. We had more than the usual anticipation for school. The 5th and 6th grades were taught by Audrey McCleary. She was a favorite teacher among the kids. She was also a very good teacher.

I was porch sitting with Mary Lee just before supper time. "Oh, Wes, I keep forgetting to tell you--remember last year when you gave me a Nancy Drew book for my birthday? It was too hard for me to read, but I got it out the other day to try it, and I can read it pretty good. I write down words for Mama to explain to me. It's all very exciting and mysterious! I love it!" A Nancy Drew fan was born!

B.J. came calling again. She said "hi" as she walked by. I walked home with her. She was carrying a fresh-from-the-oven casserole in a Pyrex dish. It smelled great!

Mama greeted her, "It looks and smells delicious! What have you created here, girl?"

"Aw, it's only a recipe I got from the San Antonio newspaper, Betty. It's called Frito Pie. I'm learning how to cook. Experimenting with recipes."

"Well, I never heard of such a thing as Frito pie." Mama was leaning over to get a good whiff of the aroma from the dish. She took three clean dish towels and wrapped them over it to keep it warm.

"I tried to get my Mama to teach me cooking. She is an intense person, impatient and sometimes her schooling was hurtful. I find written recipes easier to work with. They don't scold or intimidate me!"

Both ladies laughed at this tidbit of insight into B.J.'s raising.

"Thank you so much! I'm sure it will hit the spot. Come, sit down here. I'll get you some iced tea."

"I'm not staying, Betty. I've got one of these for Bubba and me in the oven now."

"The next time you come, we can go through my recipes and see what you might like to try, okay?

"You bet! I would love that." She hugged Mama and kissed her cheek. Very sweet.

Daddy got home soon after she left.

"B.J. brought us supper tonight, Duke. A Mexican dish that smells delicious."

"Oh, yeah! I thought I smelled something good when I came in. She's a sweet girl. Seems kinda shy to me. Like in a shell, you know?"

"I see that, too. I phoned her the other day to ask if we could be friends with her and Bubba even though we're a few years older than they are."

Daddy looked up at Mama. "They aren't young enough to be our kids, are they?"

He leaned back in his chair, stretched his arms up, arched his back and stretched his legs way out straight. Then he sat back in the chair and pulled off his boots.

"I think Bubba and I could be brothers, and you and B.J. could be sisters. There's about ten years difference between us, I guess. Seeing me and Bubba both robbed the cradle!"

He laughed at his great joke. Mama stuck her tongue out at him. I got a laugh at that.

He went on "Mostly the problem is they're a couple of love-struck teenagers who jumped the broom and now they are in over their heads, and they don't know what to do!"

"Well, speaking of jumping in over our heads, I seem to recall a bit of a rough ride for us at first. And besides, we can be a help to them sorting it out!!" Mama frowned.

"Well, you and Bobby Jo talk more than Bubba and I do about that kind of stuff. So, I'm probably wrong. I don't see why we can't all be friends. You never had a sister and neither did she. Same with Bubba and me-- never had a brother. What did B.J. think about it when you talked?"

"She said almost exactly what you just did--without the cradle robbing and in-over-their-heads part--she said the big and little brother and sister deal. They might make us feel younger, and we can help them grow up into the adult community."

The Ledbetter's invited us over for a hamburger cookout that weekend. I was already invited to eat out with the Baker family in Roca. So, I was unable to be that fly on the wall like I do so well.

But whatever they talked about over their burgers, being a "family" with them seemed to be a done deal now. I was glad of this. I liked them both and came to love them.

B.J. helped Mama in recovering of strength and vitality. Mama could nap and/or rest when she was there to watch Bella. Mama took short walks, stretching her legs and getting fresh air. And, she enjoyed B.J.'s company.

One evening later when the Ledbetter's were over for dinner and a card game, after they left, Daddy commented, "I like that young man. Must be about as talkative as I am. But he's an all right kid."

Mama nodded and smiled. "I like B.J., too. They seem to be a fit for us. We have made some dear friends at this ranch in a short while. Something that has never happened to us since we married."

"Well, now then, I have something to tell you and Wes. I didn't want to say anything with them here. They'll find out soon enough."

Mama and I were all ears. "What is it, Duke. Is it bad news?"

"No, no, Betsy, it is great news! Mr. Mac had me up to his office today at the bank. I was there most of the afternoon.

He told me his long-range plans for the ranch, and it is fantastic. So many things in the works for making improvements and upgrades. He wants my opinion and/or misgivings with every decision. We talked a long while. You know I got home with barely enough time to shower before the Ledbetter's got here."

"This sounds to me like a big overhaul of some kind. Like major changes, Duke. Does it involve Bubba somehow?"

Daddy laughed. "Come on now, Mama, I'm telling this story as fast as I can get it thought out! And, yes it involves Bubba in big way. The long and short of it is this:

Bubba is about to become the new horse trainer and livestock manager in my place, and I am already officially the Ranch Manager!"

"I will work closely with Bubba with the breeding program, horse training, and stock purchases. I asked if I could tell him tonight, but Mr. Mac wanted to do the honors. This is a major uptick for Bubba and me both. More prestige, better salary, and a lot more responsibility. And the other makeovers and changes will affect everybody at the ranch. It will take a while to get it all done--years, even."

Chapter 18

The next day I was spending some time with Mama and Bella. We were talking about the wonderful opportunity given to our family, and how excited Daddy was over his promotion so soon after we got here.

Mama was nursing Bella. She was very careful to cover herself and Bella with a light baby blanket and I turned my eyes away, too. I felt this was a private thing and I didn't need to see Mama's "ladies" anyway.

"Mama, I remember something Daddy said. What is prestige? I never heard of that."

"It means respect given to someone who has earned it. And I believe your Daddy certainly has!"

"You're right. And, I remember something now that I asked him a couple of days ago. I have been curious about it. I don't quite understand."

I had asked my Daddy some questions that fell into the "Birds & Bees" column. Not really his strong suit.

142

"Then, Daddy couldn't answer your question?"

"Well, I'm sure that he could, but all he said was that I should ask you."

Mama laughed and shook her head. "Okay, then, ask me!"

"Well, I told Daddy about getting to watch Ozzie Carmichael's cat having her kittens. It was really kind of wonderful to me, but I have questions now."

"Okay, Son, what questions?"

"Well, do dogs have puppies like that?" Mama smiled. "Yes, they do."

"And horses and cows, too?" She nodded, "Yes."

I thought for a minute, and I'm quite sure she could see the wheels turning.

"So . . . people?"

She looked at me, raised one eyebrow, and smiled again. I opened my mouth in a big "O" and sucked in a deep breath! That is how my little sister had come into the world!

Daddy had told me God put the baby into the mother. I never gave thought to how it got out! I was wading in deep water. This was mind blowing stuff. All with a few words and a raised eyebrow!

I thought some more. I had seen horses, cows, dogs, and chickens breeding, so I knew what that was. I ducked my head down for a second and then looked back at Mama again, but before I could say a word, she grinned. "Yep, that part, too."

Mama didn't get scientific or descriptive with any of it. It was explained to me as much as I needed to know at the moment. Now, I knew the importance of what the male body part was really for. It had a double duty.

I know my face turned beet red, but I was now armed with some scandalous information. I immediately told myself that I should probably never tell this to anybody.

I didn't want anyone to think my Mama would ever do anything like that. I went immediately to my room.

I was so shook up by the thought of it, I needed time to process. I decided I wouldn't even try to get help from Burley. It was just too weird to think about!

The next thing was me being mad at my Daddy because he did that to Mama.

Sometime had gone by while I laid on my bed, mulling it over. Then, a quiet tap on my door, and a sweet soft voice saying, "Can I come in?" "Yes."

"Are you okay, Wes? That was some big news for you, I know."

I nodded my head. I didn't know what to think, let alone what to say.

"Is there anything else you want to know, or something you don't understand?"

I thought Burley probably knew all of this, and I wondered why he didn't say anything to me when Mama knew she was having a baby. When I asked him, he said, "I thought maybe you needed to know, Wes, but parents are supposed to tell their kids about it. They shouldn't learn it from some other kid, or in my case from an ignorant older brother!"

I asked Mama about why she didn't tell me.

"Growing up around animals makes you learn by what you see. So, that's why you asked me and why I needed to tell you the truth right then."

"Thank you, Mama, you are always truthful with me, and I'm glad of that."

"You can always ask more about it if you want to. Anytime. Now, I'm gonna go put the beans on to heat. Daddy will be along any time now."

My darling all-knowing Mama slipped off to the kitchen. Then, common sense took over. I realized "that thing" must be what married people do to have children. God said to be fruitful and multiply, and I understood from Mama's Bible lessons this meant to have kids. Wow!!

All of a sudden, I was feeling kind of hungry, so I went into the kitchen and ate lunch with Mama and Daddy. He was home for lunch because he was now the Ranch Manager. We had a nice meal and talked like we always did. And, I wasn't mad at him anymore.

I came away feeling okay with human reproduction at an earlier age than I would have liked. I thought, "It's not a bad thing--I am starting to grow up!"

The next big event for our village community happened not too long after Bella was born. It was the strangest thing in all the history of the ranch.

Mama declared, "It's another God, thing."

It was the middle of the night only a couple of days into the New Year, January 1953. The weather was not real cold, just chilly. Mr. Tim had a dog who never missed much around camp, but it was 2:00 AM.

146

Mr. Tim didn't want to get up and go out with the dog. Ol' Pal woke him the third time in about 15 minutes, so they went out. He told us the story this way:

"I got up, put my jeans on-no shirt or shoes-and went on to the porch with Pal. He stood there listening. At first, I thought it was a cat, but then, I realized, I was hearing a crying baby. I gave Pal a sst! sound, and he jumped off the porch running."

The moon was full, so I took off after him. There it was at the base of a tree---a tiny baby, wrapped up like an Eskimo. Beside him was a grocery bag with bottles, cans of evaporated milk, and things."

"When I picked it up, the crying stopped. I grabbed the bag and went to the house. Alice was waiting. She took the baby and started to look it over good, making sure it was all okay."

"It was a bit cold on its face, and its little cheeks were red. But it seemed okay. She put a little Vaseline on in case the skin was chapped."

"When she slipped her hand into the bundle of blankets--it was warm. She changed the baby, while I got the bottle ready. We learned then that he is a boy! He ate well, burped and went to sleep in her arms."

"He's a pretty little fellow, pale skin, dark reddish fuzz on his head. He's a newborn, not much over two-three weeks old, Allie says."

"When we got into the grocery sack, Allie found a note written in Spanish and a small package wrapped in a page from the Laredo newspaper, tied with twine. It was 3,000 American dollars."

Daddy just stood there holding the telephone, as he put it, "I was dumbfounded."

Mr. Tim asked, "Duke, who do we know who can read Spanish?"

"Well, T. J. lives closest to us. He speaks it, but I don't know if he can read it."

Fifteen minutes later, Daddy was at the Jones house and T.J. was having a try at reading the note.

"This is written in an educated, very correct form of Spanish. It's not common Border Spanish. The person who wrote this came from a wealthy family, probably of pure Castilian blood. That explains why the baby looks like a Gringo. Let me translate here the best that I can."

This baby is my son, born December 10, 1952. His father was my cousin. We have shamed our family when we had a baby and no priest had married us. Our grandmother disowned us. We are rejected by all family. My cousin had some money of his own. He transferred it to a bank in Laredo. We came to the border. My cousin swam the river with our baby, left him there on the riverside, the bank...and came back for me. He was exhausted but tried to get me across. The Border police came. They tried to save us both, but my cousin, my baby's father, pushed me toward them and was washed away. They tried to find him but could not. They took the baby and me to their shelter in Laredo.

I escaped in the night. I asked strangers in the neighborhood to help me. They helped me get our money from the bank, I had papers identifying me. They took me to a truck stop. There they found a driver, but he looked like a cowboy. He told me about a ranch where he used to live. He is going to take us there. He let me write this note at a place where he bought food for me, and for the baby. He also bought more milk for the baby, and other things I need, too. He told me we would be safe at the ranch. I cannot keep this baby. You who have found my son—please give him your name, your love, and a happy life.

Mr. T. J. struggled with some of the words. "I guessed at word meanings a few times, in the context of the sentence. I think I got the gist of it fairly well."

Chapter 19

Daddy called home and brought Mama and me up to speed.

"Tim and Allie want to keep this baby. He was born December 10th. He and Bella are almost the same age. You need to fix up some diapers and other things for them. The supplies this woman had with her will be going away in a hurry."

"I need to call Mr. Mac when it gets daylight and see where we go with this. I have a peace about this situation--for Alice and Tim."

When Daddy talked with Mr. Mac, he was on the adoption plan like a duck on a June bug! "I'll get our lawyer on it. He will know what to do. We'll get a hearing right away, and then full custody granted to Alice and Tim. Some strings might need to be pulled but nothing illegal, of course. Then, the adoption will be done quicker than you can say Jack Robinson!"

After the McCleary's, our next call was to Brother Harvey. He came immediately. When he heard the whole story, he went into action. "Do you have a name for this child?"

Allie smiled at Tim. "I would like to name him after his new Daddy and my Daddy, who died last year. How does this sound: Elijah Timothy Jones?"

Tim nodded and started to snuffle, choking back tears. "We will give him our name, our love, and a good life, just like his birth mother asked."

Brother began: "Heavenly Father, by the power of your spirit we declare that this baby, Elijah Timothy Jones, is now bound to the love of God, his parents, and the fellowship of the saints. The chains of hate are broken off him in the Name of Jesus."

The entire ranch family rejoiced over this baby. God turned a tragedy into a miracle. Nobody could think of any other way for this to happen. It seemed the only explanation for Miss Alice and Mr. Tim finally getting a baby.

Little Eli had found himself a safe place to grow up with loving parents. As Mr. Mac predicted, there were legalities. Attempts made to find the mother. Odd, but the Border Patrol had no record of her.

Notices were placed in Laredo and San Antonio newspapers in English and Spanish. There was no response anywhere. Adoption plans moved forward.

The Jones family needed to get a bigger house. Their move went smoothly, and soon the new place was ready for move in. Miss Mac advised them to take a four-bedroom house She said one bedroom could be an office for Tim. Within days, Miss Allie's Mama came to live with them. A Godly grandmother to displace that awful one in Mexico.

Miss Allie quit smoking the day they got Eli. Cold turkey! She was ahead of the times with believing there was a problem with secondhand smoke. Mr. Tim tried to quit, and finally went to *Red Man* chewing tobacco.

He didn't like that it was so messy, all that spittin' and staining his mustache. The frequent stomach aches he began to have were unwelcome, too. He quit chewing and went back to smoking outside the house for about two years, but before it was over, he had it beat for good.

The winter months turned to spring. We had baby chicks and baby humans and life was good! My school life moved along, too. Final exams were upon us.

Miss Jenkins had been working overtime with Mary Lee. She told Mama, "The child is like a hungry baby bird. She cannot get enough!"

Burley and I did okay on our finals, both of us got A's. But Mary Lee was the one who knocked our socks off. When she tested at mid-term, she was below average. Now, at the end of the year, which would be her Second Grade, she was only a little below average for a Fourth Grader. She skipped most of Third Grade! She actually learned two grades in one year!

The cut off for her schooling would be when she was unable to grasp what was being taught or didn't want to go to school anymore. This year was the predicted stopping point the doctors said might happen. I thought, "We'll see about that!"

The three of us were sitting on the Baker's porch. I was watching Mary Lee. Burley was talking about something that happened in his class that was so funny. He laughed. I saw her laughing. It was no longer a silly, nervous giggle. She was at ease with the situation. She laughed because she understood the funny part.

Kids here were let loose to run around on their own. I left the house early in the morning, and sometimes it was sundown when I came home. Every Mama fed whatever kids her kids brought home. We were safe, but life is never without its surprises and mishaps.

Charlie Two Horses got stung by a wasp at the swimming hole and had to go to the hospital. The cowboys found the wasp nest, and after dark, they took a blow torch to it.

A few weeks later, Laura Hall cracked her collarbone when she fell out of a tree right in front of her house. Cookie put it in a sling, and she healed up fine.

Another day at the creek, one of the little kids went underwater and got choked. His Mama grabbed him right up, turned him over, and whacked his back a couple of times. The water came gushing out. He coughed, sputtered, started crying and screaming bloody murder. Scary, for him and his Mama, and ME-- flash back to swimming lessons.

We all ran around bare-footed, so there were the inevitable stickers in our feet, along with other cuts and scrapes. I was learning how to be a kid!

Mary Lee was right in there with us. She was free for the first time! I was glad my Mama was taking care of Bella now. She's wasn't riding herd on me like she usually did.

None of us volunteered to tell parents about all the ways other kids got themselves hurt. Mary Lee and I were both lucky, not as adventurous as others. We were careful, and at times, just chicken! But if Mary Lee did get a scratch, her Mama sort of flipped her wig at the sight of her baby's blood.

So, for the two of us, I was the medic. I got Merthiolate and Band-Aids in place to hide a small co-

co (in English "bo-bo" or "boo-boo") one of us had acquired. By the time a Mama noticed, it was old news.

One day, in the early days of summer, Mama put Bella in her stroller and went over to visit Miss Alice and Eli. They compared notes and how the babies were thriving. Mama quizzed her about how she was doing.

"I'm so glad to have my Mama here with me, she doesn't take over, but when I need her, she is right there. If I'm not knowing what to do, she is on the ball for me. If I'm pooped, she is a whiz in the kitchen, so we are well-fed."

Mama was ever the one to help people with "things." She consulted with the Lord first, then stepped into the water.

"Allie, have you given any thought to another baby? It could take a while, you know. Mrs. Mac was asking me at church Sunday if you had said anything to me."

Mama said Allie stared at her for a few seconds. "Honestly, Betty, I just took this for the miracle it is without even thinking God would do it again!"

"Well, He might not leave a baby at your doorstep again, but He could do something else. Why don't you give Miss Mac a call and tell her to put your name in the hat, again!"

As Mama told me and Daddy about this, she laughed. "Bella was asleep beside me on the couch. Allie handed Eli to me, went to the phone and got Miss Mac all pumped up! I cannot wait to see what God does to get another baby resting in the Jones nest."

Summer moved on with its usual great speed and we were coming to fall. Mary Lee was, in reality, more behind socially than scholastically at this point. Burley and I had to explain things to her.

She was more in tune socially with her age group now than she had ever been. Because she was a trooper and had some pretty good advisors!

Next up for Mama's community involvement, was a School Board meeting before the start of the school year. Mama had a mission only she knew about. It concerned Bobby Jo. When Mama got home, she told me the whole story.

She spoke about returning to work. "When school takes up, I will, of course, be bringing my baby to school with me."

Art and Music classes were only two hours, two days a week. A baby could sleep through the whole thing.

"I have developed a friendship with Bobby Jo Ledbetter. She plays the piano well and has a sweet singing voice. She would be a welcome addition to the Art and Music program."

Board members were all in favor. Board Chair Mr. Lowery met with Mrs. Mac a few days later. The Board met again. B.J. attended with Mama. More discussion and she was hired! Mama and B.J. had walked to the meeting. It was a clear night with a big moon.

The evening air felt a little cooler. They strolled along kicking around the unexpected (by B.J.) thing that just happened.

When they parted, she expressed her thanks. "Betty, I am so grateful for your friendship, and all you have done to teach me. Your encouragement and validation of my growing abilities with sewing, cooking, childcare, and now this! You have been more than a friend to me. You are my big sister."

A few days later, Miss Mac visited Mama and Bella. She was pleased with Mama getting B.J. involved at the school.

"I have been concerned when I see Bobby Jo at church. I felt she was unsettled, even with the success of her sewing business. Maybe she doesn't know how to be a wife."

"I think you are a God-send for her, Betty. And you have been a lifesaver to drift her along into a routine that she will be comfortable with."

"I can't take the credit, Miss Mac. She just showed up! And I certainly needed help with Bella! I think having someone helpless to care for has boosted her confidence. And the sewing and making her own money, was helpful, too. It's a privilege to be the tool the Lord uses to fix someone else. I think it's a ministry if we can believe it of ourselves."

"Without a doubt, Betty, it is a ministry. At times the best sermon is a life we live in full view of others: being a help to some and an example to others. That is you, my dear."

<u>*Chapter 20*</u>

[September 1954, 6th grade, 11 years old]

It was a pleasant day. I went over to see Mary Lee. I wanted to talk seriously with her.

"I want you to know that I care for you very much, and I'm glad you're my friend."

She smiled shyly but looked right into my eyes and purred, "Me too, Wes."

This was going well. "Whatcha say we walk over to Main and get us a Coke Float?"

Big smile with, "I would love a Coke Float."

I had cash from my savings with me for this occasion, just in case.

We walked along, and when we got away from the houses, I slowly reached for her hand. She gently clasped her hand with mine, like it was the most natural thing in the world. Almost seemed like she had been expecting it.

As we got closer to where people were, I let go. I didn't want anyone to see us. I didn't want any parents spying on us.

We went to the Soda Shop, and I ordered a large Coke Float with two straws. I saw that in a movie Mama took me to. The two straws thing seemed romantic to me.

We sat side by side in the booth and slurped our drink. We didn't talk much. We watched the other kids, dancing to the jukebox.

When our drink was gone, we sat back savoring the delight of our treat. Then, Mary Lee sat forward again, turned to me, and asked, "Wes, is this a date? And if it is, am I your girlfriend?"

I was blindsided by Little Miss Sunshine, and not for the last time, I can tell you! There would be much more. I struggled to have some sort of a grip, so I didn't seem like a dunce. This whole thing was just so awkward for me. I wondered how any kid ever gets through it.

"Well, you are my friend, and you are a girl. I think that means YES; you are my girlfriend. As for this being a date, why not!? Why should the teenagers get all the privileges? Why shouldn't we have a date?"

160

She did that soft hand clapping thing she did when something great happened. Her cheeks flushed a little, so I figured it was okay that my own face felt on fire like a full-on Texas summer sunburn.

I slipped out of the booth and took her hand to help her out. When we got outside, I reached for her hand again. "I am so happy whenever we're together, and I miss you when we're apart. I think of you all the time and pray for you always."

We walked toward the park and sat on one of the cement seats that encircled the big trees. I let go of Mary Lee's hand as she sat down first. Then I sat with some room between us. She immediately scooted over closer to me, and we were touching side by side.

"I think of you all the time, too, Wes, and I pray for you that God keeps you safe." I was looking at her face in profile, and with that said, she turned toward me and smiled.

I felt the anxiety building right up. I didn't know what to do next. I was so out of my depth. I wanted to be suave and in control but couldn't seem to get that done. She leaned closer and laid her head on my shoulder. She patted my arm.

"You know, Wes, I think God sent you here to Mesquite Creek Ranch to be my friend. I have never had a friend like you, not even Burley."

I took hold of both her hands, lifted them to my lips, pressing on gentle kisses. "It's time we got headed for home, and I don't want anyone to see what is going on with us until I know what to do. But I know it's important, and it is real. And, I also believe I am here at the ranch because of you."

Our eyes locked. Our noses were almost touching. Then, she stood quickly and looked down at me, the one with the rubber legs. She was the one with the smile that could melt ice off the back fence in February.

But as they say, with a voice like honey from a honeycomb, she said, "As real as Lois Lane and Superman, my dear, Wesley."

She turned, and I jumped up before she walked away from me. I thought "this went well." Yeah! It went so well; the fact of the matter was Superman was bordering on being terrified of Lois Lane. And, he could hardly keep his hands off her. And, didn't know what to do next either!

We walked home--no talking, no handholding. The sun was lowering into the West horizon. We stood on her porch facing each other and whispering about how much we enjoyed our date. I gathered her hands in mine once again, holding them, and said very softly to her, "My Sweetheart."

Then I turned around and ran to my front porch. I sat on the steps, my heart pounding, thinking about what happened. It was just about the biggest deal of my life!! I had my first date with my girlfriend who loves me. My wife to be!

I decided to tell Mama. She was drying a pie tin she had washed. She turned to face me when I came in the door.

"Mary Lee and I had our first date today. We went to the Soda Shop and had a Coke Float."

The pie plate made a clattering metallic sound when it bounced around on the tile. She smiled slightly, then bent down to pick it up. She stood up and looked at me. She just stared.

Then, she nodded, smiled and said, "I see. Yes. That's nice, Honey. I hope it was a nice time for you."

I smiled back and said, "Mary Lee is my girlfriend."

"Yes, Son, I can see that."

That night I lay in bed praying for the two of us. In a sleepy state, I began to think about being her husband, us being a family together, having children. I slept and right before time to get up, I dreamed. We were walking along the path to the church. It was a very bright sunny day. Mary Lee was dressed for church. She was wearing high heels. I had on a Sunday suit. I was pushing a baby stroller, but there was no baby. And, we were not adults. We were still 11 and 12 years old.

The next morning, it made me so happy to think about our future as I remembered my dream. I wanted to tell someone who might understand how I felt.

It was early, just at dawn. Lights were on all over the neighborhood. Cowboys getting ready for work.

I went to the kitchen. There was coffee in the pot leftover from last night. I heated it. I drank two cups, thinking and praying. Then, I got milk and cornflakes. I decided I would talk to Burley.

The sun was coming up and I heard Daddy in the shower. I dressed and shot on over to the Whitfield house. I went to the back door. Miss Whit was in the kitchen.

"Come on in, Wes. I think Burley is in the shower. Go on back and give him a hurry up."

I went toward his room and saw he was dressing. Had his shirt and pants on, working on socks and sneakers. He heard my steps and looked up.

"Wes! Here you are in the middle of the night for a visit!"

I grinned and said, "I need to talk with you, Burles."

He nodded. I told him, "My feelings are ramping up and I am having thoughts that are galloping away with me. And I told Mama that she is my girlfriend."

"What kind of thoughts? And what did your Mama say?"

"I don't know how to describe it. I want to be with Mary Lee to be very close to her, touching her. Sitting next to her. I think about her ALL the time. Mama dropped a pie pan she was washing. But did a nice recover and said she could see that Mary Lee was my girlfriend."

"Wes, you remember last year when the 6th graders went to Health Class. Did you hear anything about what we were taught?"

"Yeah, something about bathing often, eating vegetables, hand washing. Trying to stay healthy. Is that right?"

"Well, there was more to it than that. We were told not to tell you 5th graders about it. The teachers explained how our bodies change as we grow up. They talked about things you are questioning now--the feelings. There's a name for that change, the growing up thing, and the strange seeming feelings."

"I don't remember that name. It means going from a kid to a teenager. Boys will begin to have face and body hair, and girls have things too--but we didn't talk about them. That class will help you more than I can. It will really teach ones like you and Mary Lee that don't have older kids at home to tell you things. Its best you wait and learn it right. The class will start in the second 6 weeks of the year."

I was glad I had that talk with Burley. I was hearing and seeing and living the thing that has a name that he didn't remember. It's "puberty." A most extensively strange time in the life of every kid when they go through it.

Mrs. Jenkins taught the girls. Mr. Lowrey taught the boys. They both spoke to us the first week of school. They asked that we didn't talk to younger students about what we were about to learn. They said some of what we hear will not be appropriate for them. I thought of the reluctance Burley had in sharing what he did with me.

I told Mary Lee what Burley said, and even what Mama had told me. She knew some of it. But school was about to get going. Curiosity went on the back burner. But it got our full attention again when the 2nd six weeks of the semester started. We were ready to find out what the secrets were.

As it went along, I felt like it wasn't all that scandalous, Mama had told me so much already. So, for the most part it was not a big deal. Mary Lee didn't know as much as I did, but she wanted to learn, and was not feeling icky about it.

I think it helped us both to understand our maturing thoughts of each other. We wanted our time together to feel good, but not in a way that would be inappropriate.

Tricky. And our parents knew ALL about it, since they had been through it!

Chapter 21

When school got going, in choir class one day, Mama stood in front of us and motioned for Bobby Jo to come up front.

B.J. said, "Well, as you know, Mrs. Redmond, I have some news I want to share with you and the class before anyone else knows about it."

She turned to face us and said, "In four months, before Thanksgiving, I will be having a baby."

The class erupted into applause, cheers and whistling like at a football game. It was an extra fine day! I thought of Mama having Bella so soon after we got to the ranch, and Miss Allie getting her baby, Eli.

The calendar turned over only a time or two it seemed, and B.J. was not coming to school as she prepared to give birth in the Roca hospital. Her pregnancy was what they call "uneventful." Without any problems.

When Bubba walked into our classroom where we were doing art, we all knew why he was there! He was grinning from ear to ear.

"I'm a Daddy! We have a son!" O Happy Day!!! Thanksgiving was a week away, and we had so much to be thankful for.   Especially little Robert Henry Ledbetter.

Then, in due time, we took our midterm finals. All three of the Musketeers were doing well with our studies. We more or less "aced" our tests.

Mary Lee was going forward by great leaps. She had developed a wonderful sense of humor. She liked knock-knock jokes and was always laughing about something. She was the most sunny-side-up person I ever knew.

The choir got to go to a rest home in Roca to sing carols. Then we went around the town square singing for the shoppers, who joined in with us. That was really a lot of fun. Mama and Daddy were with us along with Mary Lee's parents and Mr. Whitfield.

On the spur of the moment, Daddy said, "Let's go out to the truck stop diner and see if we can cheer up some men who will be working at the last minute and trying to get home to their families in time for Christmas."

Of all the people we ever sang for, these tough hard-working men were the most receptive and grateful of all.

Some even sang with us. A few shed some tears, especially when we finished our program with "I'll be home for Christmas." We followed some of them out to their trucks as we went to our vehicles. They waved and shouted "Merry Christmas" over and over, and pulled away honking their big rig horns.

Excellent idea, Daddy. And one repeated year by year by the Mesquite Creek Ranch choir to the day of this writing.

Christmas was quiet for all the ranch. Kids were passing around cough-and-colds. But not too sick to get up early on Christmas morning for seeing what ol' Saint Nick brought to them!

The day after Christmas, I called early and invited Mary Lee to come to breakfast with my family. I wanted more than anything to TELL my parents what she meant to me.

But I felt the Lord telling me to keep quiet. My feelings were getting deeper and stronger as the days went on. But I felt it was not time yet.

I had already given Mama a warning. I think she had not told Daddy.

The breakfast went well. My parents both loved Mary Lee and were happy to have her with us any time.

She liked to come over and be able to hold Bella. She was sort of a born little mother.

The two of us sat bundled up swinging on the porch, enjoying being together. It was cold enough that we had on mittens. We didn't talk much. I had much to say, but it had to be the right time. We were still swinging, holding hands when Burley came up.

He suggested we have a checkers tournament. We went inside, played, and Mary Lee beat both of us without either of us letting her. That was a first—a big step.

She made us all grilled cheese sandwiches to celebrate her victory. It was her first time to use the hot stove and a cast iron skillet. Mama monitored.

The next week we were back in school and plunging into the Second Semester. Even though Mrs. Jenkins was not our teacher for 5th and 6th grade, she was still the one testing her progress. She decided to test her again to see what was gained in this first semester.

At the appointed time, she sent for the three of us to come to the teacher's lounge for a meeting. Miss Irene was already there.

"I wanted to tell all of you at the same time. At the beginning of school, Mary Lee, you tested ready for beginning 6th grade, right where you should be. This week you tested almost at the beginning of Seventh

Grade, ahead of schedule. This improvement is not what the doctors expected."

Burley and I were not surprised by this. We saw things that the adults didn't pick up on. Mary Lee was still learning!

Bella was growing and exhibiting her little personality, developing likes and dislikes. Mama decided we should baby-proof the house before she started crawling.

When Mama was expecting Bella, the thought occurred to me that Mercy and all her germs might be a hazard to "the baby."

Now, as we started looking for all things dangerous or potentially so, I just got it over with and asked Mama, "Will Mercy have to go outside now?"

Mama looked at me with a kind of blank expression. She smiled. "Wes, I never even thought about Mercy. She is such a part of our family. I don't think of her as a problem."

"And since we already check her close for ticks and fleas and bathe her often enough, I think Bella is strong enough to fight off doggy germs, don't you? And, I've known quite a few families that had dogs around their little kids all the time."

I was so relieved to hear this. When Bella was older and went to sleep on the rug with her blankie, Mercy liked to join her for a little power nap.

Chapter 22

Now, we were going for spring. All these months, I was having these feelings. I prayed for the Lord to help me. I did not want to do anything in my time with Mary Lee that would be wrong.

I began to hide it all from Mama and Burley. I did nothing and said nothing. I was not ashamed. I was afraid.

Then, one day I spotted Burley and Susanne Butler walking along between the houses holding hands. I stayed where I was.

They didn't see me. They went out toward the sheep pens to watch the kids grooming their sheep. I made a mental note that Burley might be the one I needed to talk to. He was far ahead of me. He had his older brothers.

It wasn't but a few days later, the two of us were riding our bikes with no one else around. We stopped for a rest under the big Mesquite trees near the creek. Then we walked down to the creek for a drink and back up into the shade.

Burley was talking about an old junker car his brothers had been working on for about a year. That morning, they finally got it started. Exciting stuff for a couple of teenagers. Now it needed some tires. And the brothers needed driver licenses.

I nodded and smiled, waiting for my chance. "Hey, Burley, I want to ask you something personal. Not for information about your privacy, but more for my own learning."

He grinned, of course. "Fire away, Champ, I got no secrets from you!"

"Well, I saw you walking along with Susanne Butler, holding hands. So, is she your girlfriend?"

Burley turned a little red and stammered---very uncharacteristic for him. Then, he stared at me, not exactly panic-stricken, but working on it.

My rock-solid, confident friend is speechless. This must be a bigger deal than I realized. And it gave me confidence that I might not be so much of a dumbbell as I thought.

"Okay, the reason why I asked you is that I want to know when it's okay for guys our age to sorta like a girl in a different way than just a friend. You know what I mean?"

He visibly relaxed. Then we both kind of laughed at ourselves. He nodded, "I do know what you mean. One day a girl is your friend, then, all of a sudden, you feel something that you never felt about her before."

"Exactly! I want to touch her hand, hug her, or put my arm around her shoulders---just to be nearer to her. And I want to know if she likes me and wants to touch."

I could feel my forehead wrinkling and I thought I was frowning.

"Well, this is all normal, Wes. My brothers say it is. And I feel the same way you do. But we have to be Godly about everything--what we do and what we think. If my Daddy found out I was kissing girls, he would likely take the belt to me."

"Wow, Burley, you're kissing Suzanne? I'm a little jealous." I chuckled.

Burley's face turned three shades of red this time, but he nervously deflected the conversation off himself and back to me.

"So, who is she, Wes?" I was taken by surprise.

"Who is the little lady who makes your poor heart thump outta your chest." And, that grin of his. Oh, boy!

"Burley, it's the only girl I have ever felt about this way. Burley---It is my sweet little sister, Mary Lee."

For a few seconds, he sat without moving or changing expression, just staring at me.

He shook his head. "Well, I can see that now. I must have been blind not to."

"That connection between the two of you, is there. If you become her boyfriend, and then later you're not, it will break her heart, and you will lose her as your friend."

"I have a commitment to Mary Lee. I will not break that. I told you I understand she may always be like a twelve-year-old. I'm not flying blind! And, besides, she is still learning!"

Burley ducked his head down. "This is some serious over-our-heads stuff, Wesley. You are scaring me half to death here! We're not old enough to think on this kinda thing."

I was exasperated now. "You don't understand. I thought you would."

"I do understand! But this way you're talking, is more than just holding hands. You've got PLANS! I don't know if you should keep it a secret or let your parents know."

"Burley, you know parents! They will say we're too young."

"Well, maybe you are!"

"Listen to me, Burley! Hear what I am saying. Mary Lee and I are going to get married when we are old enough, even if we have to run away!"

Burley looked at me like a calf staring at a new gate. He sighed.

"The first thing you need to do about all this is pray about telling Mary Lee exactly how you feel. She is not stupid! If she likes your plan, keep it quiet."

"And, see what God does as the days go by."

This made sense to me. "Okay, I should just hold her hand."

Burley nodded. "Right, Wes. Take small steps with her, so you don't spook her."

I nodded and remarked sagely, "Okay. Don't spook her."

I left Burley that day with not a small amount of confusion about spooking Mary Lee. I had no idea at all what that meant.

Chapter 23

A few days later, after school I went home, and Mama wasn't there. I figured she must have stayed after school for some reason. Grading our artwork, maybe.

So, I rode my bike over to the church. It was time to get help with all this health class stuff and the spooking of Mary Lee.

Brother wasn't there either. I sat on the steps with Mercy, waiting for him. After a bit, we both laid down and went to sleep lulled by the Mesquites whispering to the breeze.

Something woke me with a start. Mercy was standing close beside me, wagging her tail a little bit and looking up. It was dark, but there was moonlight.

I had been there for hours. I felt chilly. I looked up to see what Mercy saw. It was the form or shadow of a very big man. The moonlight at his back, his western hat put his face in a dark shadow.

I was instantly frozen with fear. I laid there, propped up on one elbow.

Just at the last minute before I died from panic, he spoke.

"What are you doing here, Son? I've been looking for you over an hour, walking all over the neighborhood. Your Mama is worried sick."

I jumped to my feet and grabbed my Daddy around the waist, hanging on for dear life. "Oh, Daddy, I'm glad to see you. I was waiting to talk to Brother and went to sleep. I'm so sorry. I didn't mean to scare Mama or make you have to hunt for me."

He chuckled, "All okay now, Wes. Let's get home to Mama."

Daddy put my bike in the back of the truck and got Mercy and me in the seat.

"Don't worry none about it, I'm glad you're safe and your Mama will be glad, too."

We rode along toward home, and then I had a thought.

"Daddy, what does it mean when somebody says don't spook 'em?"

He sat up a bit in the seat. Daddy was always glad I asked something he could answer. He had gained some new confidence when Mr. Mac made him Ranch Manager. He didn't have as much hard-physical work, but he did have a lot of responsibility. With that, came a stronger "I got this" attitude.

"Well, when we start to gentle a horse, they don't understand that we won't hurt them. Some people still tame them by bucking the wild outta them, but I much prefer to gain their trust and let them decide they want to cooperate with me. I want them to trust me, to know that I am their friend. You see?"

"When I walk up to any horse, wild or tame, the last thing I want to do is spook it. It means don't move too fast or raise my hand too quickly. I let him come to me, if possible. If I'm looking in his eye, I can usually see fear if he has any. Or, I may see a bit of a strong spirit. I remind myself to take my time and talk softly to them. You understand that?"

Boy! Did I ever! If Daddy only knew how much I understood! But my "horse" was no skittish little thing. She knew me already. As for strong spirit, yeah, I've seen that already, too.

Mama had Bella put to bed when we got home. I could tell she had been anxious. I told her about waiting for Brother and how I went to sleep.

"Do you want to stay up awhile and talk about what's bothering you, Wes?"

"I had some questions, but Daddy and I talked on the way home. I think I got the answer I was looking for."

"Okay then! Let's get you two something to eat."

The next day dawned, and the whole thing of how I felt about Mary Lee seemed to have resolved itself overnight. The anxieties were about gone.

After that, those bothersome thoughts only happened mostly when I was alone with her. But the rest of the time, when we had friends with us, I could focus on where I was and what I was doing, without thinking so much about my feelings for Mary Lee.

The school year ended right on time. We all moved on through another Texas summer. Lazy days for kids. No worries. Creek swimming.

For me, I spent the summer trying not to spook Mary Lee. After Daddy told me the skills of taming a horse, I felt like when the time was right, I would "tame" Mary Lee! And I had an idea that she wanted to be tamed!

Of course, I learned since that time, a man with thoughts like that is a "chauvinist." But back then we

didn't have much notion of that word. And, I was young-
-my motives were pure.

Impossibly, it was time for a new school year! The gang would soon be back in class. Mary Lee and I were back in class with Burley. It all kind of meshed together with Mary Lee's new school thing--her being smart as the rest of us now!

We were all making transitions. The boys were becoming much more interested in the girls, and the girls were checking us out closer, too.

For one thing, they talked to us more than usual. And at lunch, sometimes they sat with some of the boys.

I didn't understand it: the desire to connect emotionally and physically with other people was there. A feeling you don't do yourself, it just comes to you.

Women are big huggers of each other.

Boys are sort of outta luck.

Nobody had heard of male bonding or a "bro-mance."

I loved Burley almost as soon as we met, and I'm sure he felt the same. In private, we didn't reveal it much. Too creepy, I guess.

Chapter 24

[September 1955, 7th grade, 12 years old]

So, here I was with a girl that I absolutely adored. And, I wanted to tell her how I felt. I wanted to be close to her. I wanted even to plant a quick kiss on her cheek. But I didn't dare. It was all about the spooking thing!

I knew I wanted Mary Lee to be my girlfriend for now and my wife for life! I decided I didn't need someone to verify that for me. I believed God already did. But as Burley had said, kids our age--not allowed girlfriend-boyfriend status. I would have to wait awhile.

I decided, for now, I would keep my feelings to myself. I felt like my plans would seem more believable the longer I waited. If I wanted to talk, Burley was available, and he could keep a secret.

I had listened in on adult conversations forever. But now, I was understanding more of it than I ever had before. I understood things about hard times, drought, uncertain finances, and other adult themes. I picked up on certain new words.

I was becoming more curious about things they were hiding from kids. Some were things we didn't need to know yet, but once a kid like me gets on the trail of something, they won't stop.

Something very adult and shocking happened last summer. It was sort of a push into a strange reality for many of us kids. It was another step toward the harsh truths that come with life in the real world, as opposed to the ideal place where we live here at the ranch.

Our neighbors Bob and Claudine Stanton had her younger sister come for a visit. The first time I saw her, she was sitting on their front porch in the shade.

When she saw me walking to Ozzie's house, she quickly went inside. But not before I saw her face. Something terrible had happened to her. I thought she had been in a car wreck. Her face had stitched up cuts, both eyes badly swollen and black, and a big bruise on her cheek, bruises on her arms.

When I asked Mama what had happened, she turned away from me, which seemed odd. "We shouldn't butt into other people's business, Wes. We mustn't gossip."

I asked Burly if he had seen that lady. "No. But I know what happened because Miss Wilson was telling

Mama about it. That poor lady's husband beat her up. He hit her like a man fighting with another man. I almost threw up when I was listening to them talk. They didn't know I was in the house. I felt horrible about it."

All the boys talked about how any man could do such a thing to a lady. Most of us had been taught girls were fragile, and we should not ever hit them or push them down, even in playing a game.

The hurt young lady was named Maggie. She stayed with her sister on the ranch. As her bruises faded and cuts healed, she began coming to church.

She got a job at the Mercantile. One of our cowboys, Matthew McCreary, divorced and too mature for the blue-ribbon girls, began to shop often at the Mercantile. He started going to church and walking Maggie home. He began taking her out to lunch in Roca almost every Sunday. Some weeknights they sat on the sister's porch after dark. When she went back for divorce court in San Antonio, he went with her. She told the ladies all about it.

"First, Matt is a big-tall bruiser. My ex is more of a light weight and about 5'9". We walked out of the courtroom. Matt stopped as we walked by him, gave him the stink-eye, and said, *you better hope I don't ever see your face anywhere there ain't a lotta cops around. I will beat you to a pulp.* My ex went so pale! I thought he might faint."

"I asked Matt later if he meant what he had said. He tipped his hat to me, and said, Well, in theory, I did mean it. But mostly I was going for scaring the living daylights outta him, maybe treating him to a change of long johns. I have never had a fist-fight with nobody my entire life!"

Big laughs all around every time the story gets told!

They were married quickly and as the fairy tale goes, they lived happily ever after. Neither of them had children from their first marriages. Starting a family was a priority. All of us celebrated with them when a healthy handsome son was born. He weighed in at a respectable 9 lbs. 6 oz. Four other babies came along in rapid succession.

And, just like Granny's newest wool shawl, that beautiful new family was woven into the fabric of our lives here at Mesquite Creek Ranch.

This story was all the rage among us kids for weeks. The boys all thought Matt was a hero, and he was! I thought of Burley who had applied "the art of persuasive intimidation of the bully" since he was a tadpole.

Parents need to give kids as much information as they can handle. It is tricky, but it's better than leaving them without the knowledge of life's experiences.

Sometimes I asked my Daddy what a word meant, but he was uncomfortable explaining much of anything to me. I heard, "Go ask your Mama," so many times, I mostly stopped asking him. But sometimes, Mama wasn't much forthcoming either.

Most parents want to protect their children from the more brutal aspects of this world. To keep our innocence about some things. All that would show up soon enough.

Our choir program at church went well. It was Christmas Eve night with cookies and such. The service was not very long. There were gifts for kids, then folks went on home so all could get snug in their beds waiting for Santa.

We never had the jolly fat man at church. Nobody ever saw him as far as I know. True to legend, he was in and out of each house quick as a wink! And he would never upstage baby Jesus at church!

Chapter 25

Days and weeks slipped by. The weather began warming up, the cold wind was gone. One day we came in from recess where we had played dodge ball. I was a little sweaty from the exertion. I smelled something kind of stinky. I didn't know what it was.

I expected we all would keep growing and learning. But I had not thought much of the other kind of growing and development that was coming on all of us, very fast.

I kept sniffing around and finally realized the smell was coming from my shirt. I went home and told Mama what happened.

"I figured out what the smell was! Mama, it was ME!"

She kind of chuckled. "Do you know what deodorant is, Wes? It seems to be time we got some Right Guard for you."

She reached over and rubbed her finger along my top lip. "And while I'm in that aisle, I'll pick you up a razor."

I couldn't believe my ears! It was just like they told us in Health Class!

I don't remember when I became aware that women had breasts. It seemed like they had always been there. I always knew. And it didn't fully register with me that it was anything unusual. But connecting that with my female schoolmates hadn't hit me yet.

I overheard some 9th grade boys talking about a girl in their class having a "good figure." I didn't know what that was. I asked Mama what that meant.

"That means the girl's body is not like a stick anymore. Not straight up and down. She has gotten her curves."

Okay, we got "a figure and her curves" and I still don't know what that means. And, I got a sense of Mama not wanting to say more. I didn't want Mama to know I was this dumb or too curious. So, I nodded and said no more.

A few weeks after that, I remember the day—distinctly. It was a Monday morning. I was leaning against my desk before the tardy bell rang. Polly

Hanover walked in looking so nice. She seemed extra happy.

She was dressed in penny loafers, a dark blue straight skirt, and a lightweight pale-yellow sweater. I knew she had her family birthday party that weekend. I thought this outfit must have been one of her gifts.

As I looked at her, all of a sudden, I noticed her figure! I saw the curve of her hips below the waistline on both sides! Then my eyes went up, and wow! There they were, plain as day!

As I had heard, some of the boys call them: "The Twins." Much smaller than my Mama's, but they were there! I didn't say anything to anybody about it for days.

Early one Saturday morning, Burley and I took off on our bikes. We admired some wildflowers having a last bloom. We skipped some rocks at the creek. Then sat in the sun before we started home.

"Do you ever look at a girl's chest?"

Burley stared at me without the usual grin and finally said, "Yeah. At times, I do."

I told him about noticing Polly's twins and asked, "Is it a sin or anything?"

"Well, I think as we grow up, Wes, we're going to notice and think about these things that we didn't before."

"I still remember when I first noticed Miss Thompson's. She is tiny, and they are so, you know--not tiny!"

"I get that, Burley. It's hard to keep yourself from looking."

We both laughed nervously, and I realized I had noticed Miss Thompson, too, but I hadn't thought much about it.

Polly was a different story, because she was my age, in my class at school.

I was better informed but still worried. "So back to my question, is it sinful?"

"I know this: God made women the way He did, and evidently, He made men so we would notice women. If we didn't SEE them, didn't appreciate the beautiful part of them, there would be something wrong with us!"

"But I'm certain, Wes, if we think the wrong things or if we are disrespectful in our thoughts toward another person for any reason, it is wrong. We should respect all people, but especially the women and girls."

This reminded me of when I was so mad at Daddy for doing something to Mama that got her Bella. I was better informed now but the whole thing still kind of bothered me.

I wondered how you could do something that important when you don't know HOW!!!

Burley added, "And we shouldn't talk about them with other boys the way some do. They are so ignorant and trashy when they do that. I hope the Lord never lets me or you talk like that about any female person of any age! It just isn't right. One thing I do when I talk to girls--I look at their eyes."

Being such a decent kid and wise beyond his years, Burley was truly a unique individual. He stood out from the crowd for much more than being "big for his age."

I have never in my life known anybody like him or had a better friend than he is. He was my big brother from the first day we met.

Another word had popped up later when Mary Lee and I went to that Health Class as 6th graders: hormones.

It seems they cause our beards and the girl's breasts and a whole lot of other things they didn't tell us too much about.

They left a lot to our parents. Obviously, they did not take into account parents like my verbally challenged Daddy!

The next time I saw Mary Lee, Lord help me! I tried NOT to look. But when I did, there was nothing there to see. I was glad of that.

I was okay taking a quick look at the other girls, but I didn't want to do that to Mary Lee. (Not yet, anyway!)

Chapter 26

One Sunday afternoon in May, Burley and I were riding our bikes, up the hill in town, not far from the bunkhouse. We heard some kind of a ruckus over that way. We scooted over there quick to have a look-see. We stepped inside and saw Cookie lying on the floor, looking very pale and not moving.

Several cowboys were there and had sort of surrounded him. Their voices were quiet now, a low hum. Burley whispered, "If they see us, they will shoo us outta here." So, we stayed out of the way.

Back then, people didn't do CPR. The boys had a small damp towel on his forehead and a pillow under his head. One of the cowboys was pressing his wrist to find a pulse. Another said, "Somebody call Shirley Potter."

Miss Potter was a nurse. She was called upon from time to time, but usually, Cookie was the doctor. But this time, he was on the floor, completely out. And the longer he laid there, so still, the worse things seemed to be.

Miss Potter came driving her car right up to the door. She could not find a pulse either. There was nothing to do but load Cookie into the back of a pick-up. They laid him on a quilt off somebody's bed. Two of the ranch hands rode back there with him. They raced into town. It wasn't long until they had phoned the McCleary's, notifying them that Cookie was Dead On Arrival. The doctors at the hospital told the boys that he probably had a massive heart attack, dying instantly.

Mr. Mac made arrangements with the funeral home. They prepared Cookie for his send-off. Miss Mac took the funeral people one of Mr. Mac's suits for Cookie to wear. At the funeral, somebody had put one of his big wooden spoons and his stethoscope in his hands. His Bible was tucked under his arm.

The service was held at the ranch. The church was packed. Standing Room Only around the perimeter behind and on both sides of the pews. Even some folks from Roca were there, none of us knowing what Cookie must have done for them. My Daddy, Mr. Tim, and Mr. T.J. were side by side in the front row, three of the pallbearers. The other three were younger ranch hands.

Mr. Mac stood up first. "We are here today to celebrate the life of our dear friend, Jonathan Darin McTavish. Or, as we all know him, Cookie. We honor this dear man, a friend to us all. I'll start with what I know about his life before he came to the ranch."

"One night after a big Christmas party, a young medical doctor and his wife were on their way home, driving on a back road between small towns near Houston. They drove up on the scene of a one car accident. A few folks were there standing around. Ambulance and police had not arrived yet. The doctor began trying to do what he could to save the life of the most severely injured person--an unconscious 14-year-old girl."

"She was a passenger in front beside her father, who was driving. Her mother was asleep in the back seat. It appeared the driver fell asleep and the car ran into a large tree on the right side of the road. The young girl slammed into the windshield. Cookie did all he could, but she died before the ambulance arrived. Her father and mother were neither seriously injured. Both had been drinking."

"Despite evidence to the contrary, Cookie was charged with the girl's death because he had also been drinking. The family was prominent, wealthy, and demanded prosecution of the doctor. His medical license was revoked, and he did a stretch in the penitentiary at Huntsville. He worked there as a cook."

"Years later, I read in the newspaper of the disgraced doctor's soon release. I went to the prison and volunteered to sponsor him and give him a job. The doc became our cook here at Mesquite Creek Ranch."

"Cookie was twenty-five years old when he went to prison. He was forty-three when he came out. His wife had divorced him. He jumped at the chance to come to work for us. He had no family but us. For twenty-four years he was a cook, a veterinarian, and a medic at Mesquite Creek Ranch. He cared for us all. He sewed up barb wire cuts, set broken bones, bandaged up what was banged up. His most recent medical achievement was helping with the birth of Betty and Duke Redmond's first-born daughter, Bella.

"He lived a busy but quiet life. He mostly kept to himself at the bunkhouse. It was his home and the boys were his family. He never drank a drop of liquor, and never missed a Sunday morning at church. He hardly ever left the ranch. And, often said with his trademark humor there was too much temptation out there, and too much to go wrong here where he was needed.

"He was always awake and, on the job, when the gang got home after a time of honky-tonkin' and boot scootin' on Friday nights. He had scrambled eggs, homemade tortillas, and hot coffee for them.

He went to bed early Saturday nights, and the boys had better be quiet when they came in. He needed his rest so he could get to church on time the next morning." (laughs, elbowing among the cowboys.)

Mr. Mac ended saying, "He took his cooking almost as seriously as his doctoring. He served up some of the best grub I ever ate. Nobody, not even my Mackie, could beat his apple pie. I was proud to have him as my friend. He was like a brother to me."

(Long pause here for Mr. Mac to gather himself.) "I'm really gonna miss Cookie."

There were sniffles and shifting around in the seats as Mr. Mac, stepped down, and Brother Harvey stood up.

"I am also proud to have known Cookie. As most of you know, he was a deacon here at our church. And he was a fine one. He was faithful to that office and the Lord. He was my right-hand man. I know there are quite a few here today who got the benefit of his loving care and wise advice, not to mention his Dutch Uncle bawling out from time to time. (More laughter)

"He had a heart after God and was a true follower of Jesus. I'm sure some of you were led to the Lord's salvation by Cookie's life example. I wonder if anybody would care to raise a hand if Cookie prayed with you to be Born Again?"

Hands began to raise all through the crowd. It was men, mostly, a few women and teenagers.

"Cookie and I prayed together every Sunday morning before service. There were many times he called names to the Lord--his boys who were struggling. He prayed over your problems, kept your secrets, mourned your sorrows and your failures.

"He cared for each of us here on the ranch, but you bunkhouse boys were his pride and joy. You young-uns were his sons and you older boys were his brothers.

"Cookie was one of those people the Lord called "Fishers of Men." He loved to lead people to Jesus. I feel pretty sure he has done as much or more saving and dunking here at the ranch as I have!" (chuckles all around)

"Today is a special time and opportunity for us to be together with this man one last time. I recognize the Holy Spirit in this place. I feel to speak from my heart. Please listen carefully.

"If you are one of those boys Cookie prayed for and loved, but you never gave your allegiance to the Lord, or someone else here who has never accepted His salvation--now may be the time to do so.

Now, slip outta your seat and come up front here and let the Holy Spirit work in you. You can accept Jesus as your Savior and Lord and get yourself a new life. If you are already saved but feel impressed to come forward in this anointed moment to get a touch from God, please join us up here.

"Come on, right now."

At that, he beckoned with his hand. I heard boots scraping on the wood floor. I stood up immediately. Before it was over, there was a handful of cowboys young and older, several kids like me, a few husbands I had never seen at church, even some of the women, standing up front in the rarefied air of the Holy Spirit.

The front of the church was filled with people. Brother had us all repeat our acceptance of salvation, our commitment to living a Born-Again life. I had done this before, but for some reason, I felt like I needed to get in touch with the Lord, just like Brother said.

As soon as we prayed, I knew instantly that I was different. I cannot remember when I didn't know that He died for my sins. I knew He loved me. But now, I knew that I really loved Him back! If He could give His life for me, I should give mine to Him!

At age twelve, most of us have not been around long enough to be a super big sinner. But that day, I knew that I had gone to a new spiritual level, a life that I didn't have before. What a feeling!

I turned around and there was Mary Lee. She held her arms out, and I wrapped my arms around her, and we stood there hugging for a long time.

When we finally stepped back, both of us were misty-eyed. She had a glow on her face like an angel. "Wes, your face is shining!"

"So is yours! I think the Holy Spirit is on us."

Her lips parted in that angelic smile she has. She said, "I love Jesus." She nodded her head a bit and said, "And, I love you, too, Wes." Then she threw her arms around my neck again. And before I had time to think, I kissed her cheek and whispered, "I love you, too. And we really must talk about this. I want us to figure it out."

We stepped back. She put her hand over the spot where I had kissed her cheek. I saw tears in her eyes. "I know. We need to talk later." Her eyes were as blue as sapphires and as big as saucers.

My legs felt weak, quivering. When she turned and walked away through the crowd, if Burley had not come up behind me and put his arm around my shoulders, I might have fallen down right there. He held on, talking about me taking the big step, me needing to get baptized.

I wanted to tell him that I made a confession of faith and was baptized when I was six years old. I wanted to talk about what happened to me in the Lord just now and with Mary Lee. But I had to be careful. Here in this mass of people was not the right time.

"Burles, as soon as you get changed, and eat your lunch, come over. I really need to talk."

"I can see a difference in you, Wes. Your face is glowing."

His Mama called to him, and he took off to catch up with his family.

Chapter 27

So now, both my friends saw something different about me. And I saw it on Mary Lee. What can that be? I prayed silently, "Lord, what did you do with me today? I feel different, and my friends say I look different. What is this?"

My Daddy stayed behind with the other pallbearers, for closing the grave. Mama was wheeling Bella in her stroller, so I had gotten out ahead of them. When I got home, the door was locked. I dashed over to the Baker's house. She and her Mama were home.

We sat on the couch in full view of her Mama working on lunch. Then she went into her bedroom. I scooted a little closer to Mary Lee, reached for her hand.

We sat there not saying anything. I held her hand and sensed in me a very deep love for her. It seemed to be a binding connection that could be felt.

We heard Miss Irene coming back. She had changed clothes, was wearing her house slippers. More comfortable. She barely looked our way and went to making a salad--lost in her thoughts.

I wanted so much to be alone with my Darlin' Mary Lee, so I could tell her how I felt about her. Then, ask her questions about her feelings for me. We sat a few more minutes, not saying anything. I glanced out the window. Bella's stroller was on our porch. I went on home.

Mama was messing around in the kitchen in her pedal pusher pants and house shoes. She looked up at me, started to speak, then stared at me. I was headed toward my room to change before lunch, but she stopped me, came over to me. She pressed her hand against my forehead.

"Wesley, you look kind of flushed. Are you feeling well?" "Yes, Ma'am, I'm fine."

She held me by my shoulders and stared at me for a few seconds. "You went forward in the service today, didn't you?"

"Yes, Mama, I did. I felt like I was supposed to. And I felt something different."

"What do you mean by different?" "I don't know, but I can still feel it."

This went on for a while and wasn't getting much of anywhere. She asked questions, and I tried to answer, but then I didn't know the right words I needed to explain it.

Then Daddy walked in, so I took advantage of that to get away from Mama and went into my room to change out of my church duds.

But rather than getting away from the conversation, with only my dress shoes brushed and put up and me hanging up my suit coat, here came the conversation into my room. But this time, there were two of them instead of one.

We went back and forth for a while with me not knowing what to say that would satisfy them. They had questions I could not answer.

Daddy was upset and frustrated. He turned to Mama. "Can that Pentecostal thing your Mama got be inherited?"

I looked at Mama and could feel the invisible hackles coming up on her back like a wily ol' coon dog. Not a good sign.

Daddy saw it too.

He backed up a step and pushed both palms toward her. He said in a pitiful, pleading voice, "Now, Honey, I didn't mean nuthin' critical about that there, I was wondering what could have happened, that's all."

Mama marched past him and out of my room, and he trotted along right behind her. I was temporarily saved by whatever "pennacosta" was. And I now had something else to wonder about and hope to find out from Burley what it was. I had never heard that word.

Now, I heard them in their bedroom. I couldn't make out the words. Mama's voice was louder than Daddy's and high pitched. Daddy's was low, sounded calm and not angry.

It was kind of funny to me then, but later on, when I was a grown man, I thought back on days like this when I was growing up. I was married myself and, somehow, it didn't seem as funny to me anymore.

That day, listening to the two of them, I was reminded of being with Mama in a gift shop in Roca a while back. The shop was owned by an old man. Behind the counter on the wall was a sign: I am the Boss. My wife said I could be.   And the beat goes on!

Mama came out first. She began to get lunch on the table. I resumed hanging up my church clothes and got into jeans and a tee-shirt. We ate a quiet lunch—the kind where mostly nobody says anything to anybody else. Nothing was said about my "thing" that had happened. I was ever so glad for that!

Mama decided it had been a stressful day, and we needed to stay home and be quiet. Take a nap. Daddy was all over the nap part. I went into my room and got on my bed with Mercy. I must have needed a nap worse than I thought.

When I woke, the sun was disappearing behind the trees. Mercy was needing a doggy break. I took her out carrying a bread wrapper just in case. Then I saw Burley walking along with Susanne Butler.

But they didn't see me. I stood still. But it didn't matter since they weren't looking at much of anything but each other.

It made me happy to know Burley was happy. I was also thinking of tomorrow and hoping that we could talk things over and see what was what with all this. Maybe he could tell me what that "pennacosta" thing was.

I thought about the questions Mama and Daddy had asked me, and why what Daddy said got Mama so steamed. It had something to do with my grandmother.

I didn't see much of either grandparents. Daddy's sister married an Air Force man she met while she worked at Kelly Air Force Base in San Antonio. When his hitch was up, they all moved to his hometown in "upstate New York."

The sister and her family and my grandparents all lived on a farm. Daddy talked with them on the phone, but rarely. I was handed the phone to say hello to people who were total strangers to me. They visited us two times that I could remember before we moved to Mesquite Creek Ranch.

The grandparents on Mama's side were never talked about, let alone talked to. I never asked about them. I mostly didn't even think of them.

Daddy was gone and Mama was in their room. I got eggs and closed up the chickens. I was hungry, so I made myself two sandwiches with some leftover chicken. I ate a raw carrot, then swallowed a fresh raw egg. and drank a big glass of water. Once I cleaned up after myself, I took Mercy out again. Then, I went to my room got into bed again. Started to read a bit.

The next day I was awake before Mama and Daddy. My light was off and Mercy was gone, my book was lying face down on the rug. I dressed, grabbed a banana, and went out to find Mercy.

She was on the porch waiting for me. Lights were on in the Baker house, but I had no way to know if anyone was awake. It was still dark except for the moon.

Everybody had their windows open now taking in the breezes. I crept over to the side of the house where

Mary Lee's room was. I called her name, trying not to be too loud.

Finally, she raised up in the bed. "Who is that?"

"It's me, Wes."

She came to the window, but I still couldn't find a way to tell her my long-range plans.

Finally, I asked, "Mary Lee, what do you see for us in the future?"

"Oh, Wes, don't be slow about this! We'll get married, of course!"

Okay. What happened? So much for Miss Slow Learner!!

When I was too blind-sided to speak, she went on, "I know you may not want to saddle yourself with someone as slow-witted as I am, so if it's a problem, I think you should tell me now."

She paused, I guess giving me a shot at speaking. I'm more of a talker than my Daddy, but there are times when I seem to be more like him than I think I am.

She continued, "I will need a husband who understands my handicaps and is willing to help me through all that. And I will definitely want babies. If that's a thing you don't see for you, then you need to say it now. And we can just be friends."

I felt like we were in a swimming pool, she just dunked me and was holding my head under. Suddenly the realization hit me, I needed to match wits with this girl/woman, or she was going to roll over me like General Sherman over Georgia.

I found my tongue and my moxie. "Mary Lee Baker, I most certainly want to marry you and have kids with you!!"

I paused for a deep breath and wondered what to say next. Then, blurted out, "I will have to figure out what I can do to make us a living. I would like to stay on the ranch here where we have a lot of support from our parents and friends. And as for you being slow-witted, that is most certainly NOT true anymore!"

"You have proved over and over that you can learn, and you remember. I am so happy for you, and you should be proud of yourself and what you have done in school. Never say anything again about not being smart, and--I mean it! Miss Jenkins told us when she gave you the last test that you are way ahead of your grade level!"

She got all excited, and I had a time getting her to keep her voice down. "Wes, I am so happy that you want to marry me. I love you so, so much."

"My Sweetheart, I don't think I could love you any more than I do, but I am going to try!! I need to go home now and let Mama know where I am and then I have some stuff to do with Burley. I'll come back after a while, and we can take a walk down to the creek. And maybe find a quiet spot to talk over our plans."

About that time, I saw light coming in as her bedroom door was opening slowly. I ducked straight down out of sight under the window.

I heard Miss Irene. "I thought I heard voices. What are you doing there, Mary Lee?"

I was shocked when Mary Lee answered with no hesitation. "Oh, good mornin' there, Mama. I was looking at the stars telling them to fade away, so the sun can come on up."

I heard her Mama walking towards the window. I skedaddled around the corner of the house into the dark as fast as I could go. I made a mental note that this clandestine stuff was going to be a real pain in the neck the older we got.

Chapter 28

Right when school was about to start, the community was blessed when Miss Allie and Mr. Tim got the call from Miss Mac that there was a baby available for adoption at the Roca Grande hospital. Miss Mac had few details.

"The baby is two days old and healthy. That is all the information the hospital attorney had. He didn't know race or even gender. The mother was a 14-year-old girl. Her parents want a closed direct adoption. Neither party will ever know the identity of the other."

"I know its short notice, Alice. And, with Eli not out of diapers yet, if you want to hold off, they have other options. I was their first call. But if you are ready, you can pick up this baby tomorrow."

Allie did not hesitate. "Normally, I would want to talk it over with Tim, but this time I think it will be safe to answer for both of us. Yes, we will take this baby."

The next day Allie and Tim were home by 3:00 PM with their baby! She has light brown hair, appears to be Caucasian. She is Patricia Annette Jones. Or, Patty.

Our attention was turned to gearing up for school. The usual shopping and so forth. Mama and I had it down to a science now! We got it done in one trip.

I walked over to check in with Burley. I had not forgotten the Pentecostal thing or the Mary Lee thing. With her, I had taken my thoughts into captivity, like the Bible says.

But the curiosity about Pentecost was with me almost daily. I held my peace, waiting for the right time.

Burley was under the overhang of The Shed--his Daddy's workshop. Horseshoeing tools, oil change items, other odds and ends were around the shop floor, hanging from hooks and peg boards, or up on shelves. Burley had his bike wheels off and was cleaning the chain and other parts.

"Hey, Burles, what you got going on with your bike?"

"Good Morning to you, Wes! It's not much of anything. I wanted something to do that was in the shade. I heard about the new Jones baby."

He smiled, then laid the bike chain down. "What's wrong, Wes?" He could read me like a book sometimes.

213

No one else was around, so I decided this was that time. I asked him if he knew what "pennacosta" means.

"Well, yes, I can explain that I think. It's actually pronounced Penta-cost-tal, from the Greek word pentecost. It's a Jewish feast written about in the Book of Acts. Where did you hear about it?"

"I know something changed in me, Burley, at Cookie's funeral. And I know my grandmother, Mama's mother, must have believed this way. I think I may have got the Pentecostal power."

"After Cookie's funeral, at home, Mama looked at me and thought I might have a fever. Then, she started to quiz me about what happened when I went forward. I was trying to tell her, but I didn't even know myself what had happened to me. I think she saw something."

Burley's brow furrowed, "I remember the glow on your face. I had forgotten about it."

"Yeah. Well, Daddy came home, and I went into my room. Before I could even change out of my dress clothes, they both came into my room and stared at me and went on with the third degree. Then Daddy asked Mama a question about Pentecost and my grandmother. Mama stormed out hopping mad, and he was following after her saying he was sorry, sort of whining that he didn't mean anything bad. It was crazy! I've heard Daddy say things to Mama about her mother. Now, I wonder if my grandmother and maybe even Mama, are Pentecost people."

Burley nodded seriously and opined, "It wouldn't surprise me."

I jumped in with both feet, "Burley, do you believe in this Pentecost?"

His grin was bigger than usual, "My friend, I am a tongue-talking, died in the wool, Holy Roller, for sure! My granddaddy is a Pentecostal preacher. My family doesn't noise it around because people like your Daddy and my Mama don't understand. The Bible says we shouldn't do things that would offend other people."

"Explain it to me, Burley. Tell me what the Bible says about it."

"Sure! After Jesus rose from the tomb, he was about to go back to heaven. He told his followers to stay in Jerusalem until they got power from on high. Some people say this power isn't for today. But Pentecostals believe if they needed that power back then, we need it even more today!"

"On the day of Pentecost, they received something different from salvation. They call it a "Second Touch" of the Lord. The first touch is on the inside when we are Born Again with salvation."

I was getting excited by what I was hearing. "I know I had the first touch, but I think maybe what happened at Cookie's funeral was the Second Touch for me."

"Well, the Second Touch, or The Anointing, is on the outside. It has power to give great courage and the power to speak out for the Lord, preaching, praying, and ministering to others. Usually salvation is not so visible, but The Anointing is."

"Oh, Burley, that's why my parents saw something different about me! Even my Daddy was guessing that is what it might be, and he doesn't even believe it!"

"I am so happy for you, Wes. And receiving from God the way you did without anybody else explaining it or teaching you about it!! For me that is positive proof that it is real. You know it isn't something you made up yourself."

"God anointed those Believers for His service, and He gave them the ability to speak in languages they had never learned. That's what Pentecostals believe. And it has been happening somewhere around the world for two thousand years!"

"It is clear to me that you got the Second Touch, also called the Baptism in the Holy Spirit. And there is no doubt that God has a definite plan for your life. I think you should talk with Brother Harvey about all this, and maybe about Mary Lee, too. I am sure she is part of your plan, too."

I grinned. "Well, she got the Second Touch, too, just like I did. So . . ."

Burley started laughing, and it made me laugh, too. God was up to something here!

The next Sunday after church service, I asked Brother Harvey, "Could I have some time with you tomorrow after school."

"Absolutely, Wes, come on by. I'll be here."

At home I let Mama know. "I'm going tomorrow to visit with Brother, and you don't need to worry about me this time, because I have an appointment. And, I'll be home way before dark." We both laughed.

I went over to the Baker's. Mary Lee fixed us a snack: bologna tortilla roll-ups, cheese cubes and celery sticks. Then, we walked over to the sheep barns. There weren't too many kids around. I had been thinking about what I wanted to say to her now. I remembered the part about not spooking her.

I began carefully, "This thing between us is kinda over my head. I don't know how our friendship will work now that it's out in the open--us getting married and all that."

217

"What do you think about us being in love? We can belong together in secret. Not talking about it to friends or parents yet. I don't want them to make us stop being friends. What do you think?"

We sat in silence for a bit. I wondered if she heard what I said. Then she said. "You want to go back to your house and play checkers?"

"Yeah, that's a great idea." I didn't know what this meant.

When I met with Brother Harvey, it was all about Pentecost.

"Brother, I want to know about Pentecost. I talked with Burley about it, but he thought I needed advice from you. I was Born Again and baptized when I was younger. This was something else, at Cookie's funeral when I went forward. I felt different. It was like I went into another place with the Lord. I felt Him in a way I never had."

"I have more understanding of what sin is. I know not to lie or steal, that kind of thing, but this is more. Now that I think about it, it seems as if it was a sort of protection came over me to help me be steady on with Jesus, and not sin."

"Wesley, this is what we refer to as a call on your life or the Baptism in the Holy Spirit. Like the people on the day of Pentecost in Acts. Jesus explained to them to wait for the power. There were several people at the funeral that day who were touched by the Lord. But I feel sure you were the only one who got the holy zap!"

"My Grandmother, Mama's mother, is a Pentecost person. I heard my Daddy talking about it, and I know he doesn't like it."

Brother nodded, "Well, yes, it is important to obey the Lord. But we also must respect our parents, even when we are grown, and even if they are wrong. So, it's kinda like walking the top rail of a fence and trying not to fall off! The Lord will guide you."

I was so relieved to hear this. I was not sure enough what this was all about to try to explain it to my Daddy. And if Mama had ever explained it to him, he didn't seem to have gotten the gist of it.

Brother said kindly, "You have a call on your life, Wesley. It's more than many adult Christians ever accept. We are all called, but only a few of us step up to accept being chosen. This will work itself out. Don't stress or try to fix it yourself. Let God lead you."

"Brother, I want to meet with you again and bring my Mama. I want her to talk about this, where she is with it and what she thinks about me being in it."

219

Brother chuckled. "Wise of you, young man. Just let me know when."

I stood and shook Brother's hand, "Thank you for all you do for me, Brother Harvey."

He smiled, "You bet! Keep in touch with me, Wes."

"Oh, by the way, Sir, there was one other person who got the holy zap."

"Really? Who was that?" "It was Mary Lee Baker."

Before he could get over his obvious surprise, I slipped out the door.

Chapter 29

[September 1956, 8th grade, 13 years old]

It seemed over summer all three of us grew in height. Daddy measured us up against the doorpost. Burley was 6'2" same as my Daddy. I was 5'9". Mary Lee was 5'6".

It felt impossible there was another year of school already. But it was Monday and school was in session. I was lying across my bed in my PJ's when the school bell started ringing. I had never been more disinterested in school in my life! The Lord reminded me of Jesus in the temple, wanting to hang out with the wise teachers and "be about his Father's business." But He had to go home with his parents. I laughed at myself and decided I should get to the kid stuff I still needed to do.

Mary Lee and I walked home after school. Burley was nowhere around. There was homework that first day! Reading. We each changed clothes, did the reading and met outside for a walk to the creek again. I told her about honoring our parents and not causing them grief by flaunting our experience that they did not understand. "God will work this out so our parents will have their hearts prepared and when it's the right time, they will accept what the Lord is doing with us."

She agreed with this and I felt peace. She wanted to talk to Brother, right then. So, we went over to his office. She didn't mince words. "Brother Harvey, I'm sure my folks will not easily accept the Pentecost thing. Explain to me what you told Wes about honoring our parents."

As they talked on, she told Brother we were planning to get married. He listened and kept the straightest face I ever saw. No blink, no shock at all.

"I think the most important thing now, is that you both remain obedient and Godly in all things. Honor the things your parents ask of you until you are grown and can make your own decisions. Be careful about what you tell them that they may not understand."

He paused and looked at us. He sighed a little and added, "Especially the part about you getting married."

When we stood to leave, Brother had that serious look. "The Lord impresses me that I must tell the two of you one more thing: And this is so important! Please--- listen----carefully: You must keep yourselves pure and wait until you are married to become husband and wife. Do you understand what I mean?"

The two of us looked at each other. Mary Lee's face turned beet red. I was pretty sure mine had gone ghostly white. We both looked up at him and said, in unison, "Yes, Sir!" Then we turned and ran out the door as fast as we could go.

Later, when we told Burley what all Brother said to us, it triggered some problems for him, about his girlfriend.

"I like Susanne, and when I saw she liked me too, I was so happy, you know. But the more I have been around with her, the more I get a feeling the Lord is speaking to me about her."

He was conflicted, obviously. "Susanne likes to kiss too much, and she wants us to be alone. That's the reason why I haven't seen as much of you two lately."

"And then there's another thing. I have something from the Lord that may not be exactly like you two. But it's my calling. I need to figure out what it is--my future."

"Burley, we are with you and want you to be happy and in the Lord. But it sure seems like He is showing you that Susanne is not the girl for you. Because we have given our lives to Jesus, we have to be careful who we get close to. Brother Harvey said that."

It was less than a week later when Susanne, without so much as a "so long, it's been nice to know ya" was walking along Main Street holding hands with Carl O'Brien. It was a fine how-dee-do! And just like that-- Burley was on his own. But he was fine with it. The three of us had talked things through with Brother and each other.

Our hearts were more settled now as we were going toward whatever the Lord wanted for us, and what our next year of school might bring.

The next Sunday evening the Three Musketeers were on my porch. Burley was feeling fine and ready to talk.

"I saw Brother in the hall after services, and he asked me what was going on with me. I told him I needed an appointment with him. He smiled a little and nodded his head. He took a deep breath and said we should get to it!"

"We met this afternoon, and he plunged in before I could say anything. He feels there is a call on my life. Then, out of the blue, he asked if there are any preachers in my family."

"Whoa, Burles! Heavy! I'm glad to hear this."

He grinned. "I told Brother the whole story of Daddy being raised in Pentecost, but not going to church anymore."

Mary Lee and I were about to learn some facts neither of us had ever heard.

"My parents met at a bowling alley. My raised-in-church Daddy got carried away with this feisty young girl. She was not like anyone he had ever known. He was sheltered from worldly things. They ended up getting married at City Hall. She didn't believe in God. Daddy said he forgot to ask her about that before they tied the knot."

"Both of Mama's parents were drunks. She was the oldest kid and was taking care of the others when she was a kid herself. To get away from it, she married the first country bumpkin that came along."

Burley's Daddy explained things to his children: "When you babies came, Mama felt like she was right back where she started, taking care of kids and not having much fun. She loved you guys but wanted something more. Plainly, what she needs is Jesus!"

"He went to church with us kids, taught us salvation in Jesus. When we got older, he told us that people who don't have Jesus, always feel an emptiness inside. Their life is always missing the necessary ingredient for happiness. That's why your Mama is so miserable."

Burley smiled sadly, "But, she has never wavered from her unbelief. She doesn't object to us believing. She drinks. And that may lead to a big meltdown fit. She's a three pack a day smoker, too."

"All of this grieves Daddy, but he stuck around for us kids, and he loves Mama. She hasn't been a totally bad wife and mother. She cooks, keeps a clean house, does laundry, and pays attention to us kids when she's sober enough, and even seems to love Daddy."

"Then I told Brother Harvey about my Pentecostal Granddaddy preacher. That opened up a whole new ball game! Brother said he got a strong feeling from the Lord about the call on my life."

"He said it might happen that my Granddaddy is praying for me to answer the call that has by-passed my Daddy because of his situation. My Mama may have hindered Daddy from pursuing his first calling."

Burley smiled at us, "My heart started pounding hard when Brother said that, I thought I might pass out. You two know that I think preaching is my calling."

"Burles, no surprise to us. You have a pastor's heart--been taking care of me and Mary Lee for years! A flock of two! And you know the Bible better than any kid I ever saw."

Mary Lee chimed in, "But first we need to get you out of school!"

Keeping our eye on the ball with school was a must. Before we knew it the Thanksgiving-Christmas holidays were over. We had a semester left to squeeze the goodness out of this year before it was over. This school year was a pivotal time for Mary Lee and me. It is technically the last grade in "grade school."

The Ninth grade is actually the Freshman year of High School. Miss Jenkins alerted us to this truth. She spoke to us at the end of school last year.

"I advise you to do as much reading as possible from the Required Reading List, provided to both 8th and 9th graders. It is required in 9th grade that you have read eight books on the list, but the more you read, the better prepared you will be for High School." I read seven books in 8th grade, and five in 9th grade.

We were serious about education, but it was important to be cool. The right kind of clothes was a big deal in this stage of teen development.

First. there was one brand of jeans in rural Texas that "real" cowboys wore almost exclusively, to the point it was a cultural must. That brand still dominates and will be worn by the next generation after this one. For the younger kids, our mothers bought us the cheapest brand of jeans and plain cotton T-shirts.

This year, when Mama declared shopping for school clothes day, I told her I would like to start dressing like the older boys.

"Are the boys your age doing that now? I hadn't noticed."

"Well, the ones with older brothers do. Burley was wearing western shirts and Wrangler jeans last year. I didn't say anything because we had already bought my school clothes. But now, I'm thirteen years old--not so much a little kid anymore."

Mama seemed to pull out all the stops when we shopped. I got two pairs of Wranglers and cloth for making long sleeve western shirts. Mama thought I needed a new belt, this time real tooled leather. And she also bought a genuine suede leather jacket.

She starched and ironed the jeans and shirts just like she did Daddy's. I would hang up my Wranglers after school for wearing two or three times before they were washed. Mama washed my shirts by hand, to keep them from fading fast. I was ready for school now!

The first day of school I was dressed in all my finery. I checked Mama's big dresser mirror and liked that guy looking back at me! Mama smiled when I walked into the living room.

"Well young man, don't you look like a million bucks!"

I had on my first ever pair of Justin Roper boots. For several days I had walked around the house to break them in a little. They made me feel like I really belong here on this ranch. They made me taller, too.

Another change was my hair. Mama smoothed on a dab of Daddy's hair oil. She parted my hair and combed one side into a wave. "You're too grown up and handsome now to wear kid bangs in your eyes like Dennis the Menace on TV!"

I was standing on the porch, waiting for my two best friends. They were walking toward me. As I went down the steps and into the sunlight, Mary Lee stopped and gasped out loud. She squealed, "Wes, you are beautiful!"

Burley grinned big and chimed in immediately, "Yes, you are!"

Never in my short little life did I feel so good about ME. My confidence level shot up about a thousand points. Three people who love me most in this world told me I was "something else!" I was handsome. I was beautiful. Not to mention I was in style, and pretty smart, too!

As we got to school, kids were milling around outside, waiting for the bell. I saw admiring looks from the girls. The boys were smiling, too, elbows digging at each other. A few whistled, others were saying, "Whoa, Wes, what's going on!" and "Great new look, Wes Man."

I thought, "What could be better than this??" That day is still high on my list of all-time memorable moments. I was so heartily admired by my friends. Not many things in life can beat that kind of validation and acceptance.

After these thoughts warmed my heart, I had sense enough to tell Mary Lee and Burley how great they looked, too.

"My sister and my brother, if there are three best friends in this entire school who are better looking than we are, we Musketeers must immediately challenge them to a duel!"

We were laughing as we walked up to the steps into the school building like comic book superheroes. It was Burley and me with Mary Lee between us and the other kids moving aside letting us walk through. Much camaraderie and shared joy among us.

Life for me had never been so good

as it was that day at

Mesquite Creek Ranch